"I love babies,"

Wren told Blake. She stood still, gazing into some memory, her lovely profile clearly defined in the dusk that filled his office. When she moved again, it was with conviction.

"And I want at least four of my own, in a big, two-story house full of baseball mitts and tap-dance shoes and bicycles and miniature cars and—"

"Wren...?"

She snapped to a stop at his solemn inquiry. If he hadn't spoken, she would have charged right into him, which he realized, too late, would have been far less dangerous than where she'd stopped, just a few tantalizing inches away.

Against every ounce of his will, his gaze strayed to her lips. He knew then that he wanted to kiss her, that he'd wanted to for a long time....

Dear Reader,

Babies—who can resist them? Celebrating the wonder of new life—and new love—Silhouette Romance introduces a brand-new series, BUNDLES OF JOY. In these wonderful stories, couples are brought together by babies—and kept together by love! We hope you enjoy all six BUNDLES OF JOY books in April. Look for more in the months to come.

Favorite author Suzanne Carey launches the series with *The Daddy Project*. Sherry Tompkins is caring for her infant nephew and she needs help from the child's father, Mike Ruiz. Is marrying Mike the best way to find out if he's daddy material?

Lindsay Longford brings us *The Cowboy, the Baby and the Runaway Bride*. T. J. Tyler may have been left at the altar years ago by Callie Jo Murphy, but now this rugged cowboy and his adorable baby boy are determined to win her back.

Lullaby and Goodnight is a dramatic new story from Sandra Steffen about a single mom on the run. LeAnna Chadwick longs to stay in the shelter of Vince Macelli's arms, but the only way to protect her child is to leave the man she loves.

The excitement continues with *Adam's Vow*, Karen Rose Smith's book about one man's search for his missing daughters—and the beautiful, mysterious woman who helps him. Love and laughter abound in Pat Montana's *Babies Inc.*, a tale of two people who go into the baby business together and find romance in the process. And debut author Christine Scott brings us the heartwarming *Hazardous Husband*.

I hope you will enjoy BUNDLES OF JOY. Until next month—

Happy Reading!

Anne Canadeo
Senior Editor
Silhouette Romance

Please address questions and book requests to:
Silhouette Reader Service
U.S.: 3010 Walden Ave., P.O. Box 1325, Buffalo, NY 14269
Canadian: P.O. Box 609, Fort Erie, Ont. L2A 5X3

BABIES INC.

Pat Montana

Silhouette
R O M A N C E™
Published by Silhouette Books
America's Publisher of Contemporary Romance

To my mother,
who always thinks I can,
and to Frank and Kyle,
who taught me the miracle of life.

 SILHOUETTE BOOKS

ISBN 0-373-19076-X

BABIES INC.

Copyright © 1995 by Patricia A. McCandless

Printed in U.S.A.

Books by Pat Montana

Silhouette Romance

One Unbelievable Man #993
Babies Inc. #1076

PAT MONTANA

grew up in Colorado, but now lives in the Midwest. So far she's been a wife, mother of four adopted daughters and a grandmother. She's also been a soda jerk, secretary, teacher, counselor, artist—and an author. She considers life an adventure and plans to live to be at least one hundred because she has so many things to do.

Some of the goals Pat has set for herself include being a volunteer rocker for disadvantaged babies and teaching in the literacy program. She wants to learn to weave and to throw pots on a wheel, not to mention learn French, see a play at the Parthenon in Greece and sing in a quartet. Above all, she wants to write more romances.

Dear Readers,

For me, the joys of motherhood arrived in something other than a tiny red-faced bundle of potential just waiting to be molded. Instead, I received four very beautiful and already clearly defined young ladies—Julie, Patti, Marci and Jan—who were fifteen, thirteen, nine and seven and not at all sure what they would do with a stepmother who cooked Swiss steak with green peppers when any mom with a lick of sense would fix hamburgers and potato salad…and chocolate-chip cookies for good measure.

But they were tolerant and patient and accepting, and over the years I learned beans 'n' wienies…and the art of listening…and the many facets of love. Today I am the proud adoptive mom of these daughters who were born not under my heart, but in it.

From them came smaller packages—the miraculous bundles of joy that are my three grandsons, Frank, Kyle and Joe. They taught me what I needed to give life to little Ryan in BABIES INC.

It is an honor to be one of the first in the new BUNDLES OF JOY series. Writing this book gave me the pleasure of creating characters whose capacity to love extends beyond traditional roles. Single father, aunt, guardian, ward, foster child—titles really don't matter as long as hearts have endless love to give.

Warm regards,

Pat Montana

Chapter One

"*Babies?*" Blake Brockman thundered.

Wren March's determination wavered at the storm threatening in her boss's usually well-controlled baritone. She'd already had to deal with Blake's hair-trigger mood more than once this morning, and this was only Saturday! Heaven only knew what would break loose when she told him about Monday.

"You don't like babies?" she asked lightly, ignoring the file marked Denver Airport lying, corners squared, next to the other neatly stacked folders on his always-orderly desktop.

She watched Blake shove long fingers back through the shock of honey-blond hair that fell across his tanned forehead when he was irritated. It was a familiar gesture, reminding her that Blake's squalls rarely blew into a tempest.

But she wasn't sure this time, and his answer worried at her heart. Did Blake *really* not like babies?

Blake's blue eyes darkened like a sky going to storm. Everything about him, from the lines of skepticism in his broad forehead to the downturn at the corners of his full mouth, shouted his answer.

He stood abruptly, his lean frame looming over the desk. "What I think about babies is irrelevant, Wren." Plunging his fists into the pockets of his charcoal-gray cords, he paced to the windows of his Cherry Creek office.

Wren used the moment to recapture her breath, certain that whatever Blake glowered about wasn't the snow-covered mountains to the west.

When he turned, she wasn't surprised to see he'd regained his composure. Even his hair lay smoothed into place as if by the sheer strength of his will. Only the silver key he burnished in his fist hinted at barely subdued force.

"The point is, Wren," he said, sliding the key back into his pocket, "the baby market has already been overresearched." His voice projected that cool firmness that told her his mind was made up.

"The airport account is new . . . and big. I need everybody, including Wren March, working on it." Fixing her with unyielding scrutiny, he picked up the airport file and thrust it at her.

Wren hitched herself up taller in the chair and accepted the file, swallowing the knot of disappointment in her throat. His unspoken command told her that nothing had changed. At least, not for him. But, darn it, things *were* different now.

"Blake, I am not your part-time gofer anymore. Monday I'll be a full-fledged market researcher." Boldly she laid the file back on his desk. "There's a baby boomlet going on out there—haven't you noticed? There are pregnant women everywhere ... and babies all over TV. It's an epidemic. It's in the water.

"Besides ... I think I have a client." She sat forward, anticipating his approval.

"You've been soliciting clients?" Approval was definitely not what boomed in his voice.

"No, the client came to me," she announced proudly, but his face remained as stony as Pikes Peak. He apparently wasn't going to give her a standing ovation. "One of the women I graduated with is expecting, and her father owns a company called Nestlings and he asked her what she thought about—"

"Wr-en." Blake cut her off with that bloodless execution of her name that made him sound like a disapproving big brother. It warned her that he'd shifted into his unbearable "older and wiser" routine. She braced to endure the inevitable lecture. It wasn't long in coming.

"You insisted on getting your degree in the business, and you seem intent on working in *my* business. Let me remind you that just because Aunt Ruby gave you a few shares in my company does *not* give you the right to create your own clients."

He rested his broad palms on the top of the desk and leaned menacingly toward her, brows gathered over his shadowed blue eyes. "If you're not going to work on the airport account, then maybe you'd better think about finding yourself another boss."

Wren's heart plummeted. The immovable Brockman...still treating her like a pesky little sister, like the teenager his father had pressed him into hiring four years ago.

She'd thought, after graduation, that he'd get around to realizing she was a woman. Darn it, she *was* a woman—she was almost twenty-three—and it was high time Blake stopped acting like some remote patriarchal guardian. He was acting too much like his father.

"I didn't know marine training passed down through the genes," she answered tartly.

Blake stiffened. "The Colonel may be my father, but that's where the resemblance ends."

There was that rumble in his voice again. Blake might disclaim a likeness to the Colonel, but some days he even *sounded* like him. But she had no intention of letting Blake continue in the errors of his father's ways.

"Just give me a chance, Blake. Let me show you a proposal for Nestlings. If they don't buy my suggestions, I'll do the airport job. I'll even work with you on weekends."

This problem of not being able to breathe while she waited for his answer was getting to be a nuisance. Things would be much worse, though, if she couldn't sway him to her plan. She'd have to go back to square one.

"A chattery self-willed female who refuses to be fired and wants to hang around on weekends to update me on the latest sitcoms? Forgive me if I don't consider that a very good bargain, Wren."

Blake sat down, his stormy blue eyes still stern, but she could tell by the softening of his mouth that he'd relented.

Another man existed behind Blake's seldom-smiling face, and that man's intensity was in serious need of redirection. The thought restored Wren's determination.

"You won't regret it, Blake, I promise. You'll get more than you bargained for."

"You always provide more than I bargain for, Wren."

Though his words still held an edge of sarcasm, his eyes lightened with amusement, expanding her heart as if it were a balloon. She knew he would at least consider her ideas, if only because she was a hard worker. Blake might be a curmudgeon at times, but he was a fair and considerate boss.

"But I don't need any more surprises," he added. "Just put that college education to use and come up with a professional proposal. I'll take a look at it...but don't get your hopes up."

Don't get your hopes up. Blake was much too late with that warning. She never relied on hope. Her father had taught her that her namesake was a feisty little bird given to fighting for what it wanted.

What she wanted was to hang on to the nest she'd built here at Brockman Incorporated. Beyond that...well, she knew it would take work as tough as moving a mountain, but she was going to become Blake's partner.

She wasn't a kid anymore, either, and she intended to make him realize that, too. *That* would take moving the very earth under his feet.

She'd need some pretty powerful magic to budge the immovable Blake Brockman. Fortunately, she knew exactly what to use.

"Come on, Wren. I'll show you your new location." Blake preceded her into the hall, relieved to be out of close quarters with her.

For some reason, Wren bothered him more than usual today. It wasn't her frequent laughter or her unrelenting optimism, or even the fact that she always forgot to call him Mr. Brockman at the office. He'd gotten so he could ignore those most of the time. Nor was it the rippling brown ponytail swaying at her shoulders, he mentally ticked off. He'd been the one, after all, to allow casual dress for the telemarketers. Even the jeans and oversize purple sweatshirt she wore with the crazy green frog on the front didn't get to him. Too much.

Nothing had changed. She was the same little Wren. So what was his problem today?

"Hey, Mr. Brockman, are you moving the Bird Woman out on us?" Jaime Sandoval intercepted Blake before he could hurry Wren past the telemarketing cubicles.

Wren stopped at the cubbyhole next to Jaime's and picked up a briefcase. Blake detected the warm earthy scent of new leather—probably a graduation present. He watched her stroke its smooth brown surface and thought how closely it matched the color of her eyes. The thought startled him.

"Hey, Wren, we'll miss you."

"Moving up to the big time, little lady?"

"What are you doing here today?"

Blake wondered the same thing while he waited for the telemarketing staff to greet her. He nodded to the high-energy college students—so like Wren, so terribly young—and to the retirees, relaxed and comfortable in contrast.

"I'm not leaving, Martha," Wren answered. "We can still take breaks together."

"*I* won't miss you," Jaime said, grinning up at Wren. "Maybe now some of the rest of us can win the weekly quota incentive. I still expect lunch with you Saturdays, though. Including today."

Blake didn't remember Jaime ever annoying him before. Today everything seemed to chafe.

He moved ahead, his patience with the friendly banter nearly spent. "Your new desk is back here, Wren." He led her out into the main work area, past the four desks in the middle, to the lone desk in the far corner.

"This is mine?"

"All yours."

When she turned to look up at him, he was reminded of the first time he'd ever seen her, when the Colonel had become her guardian and she'd moved from the small mountain town of Antler. She'd been so small…a little moppet of a thing whose father had recently died. Whose mother had run out on the two of them long before that.

He'd felt sorry for her then, with those big eyes and plain hair, even while he'd resisted his father's request to help out with her care.

He'd felt sorry all right…until she'd opened her mouth. That was when he'd realized that the top of her head might not come to his shoulders, but this was one moppet who could take care of herself.

She'd been fifteen then, and she was hardly any bigger now. She'd been his best phone researcher ever, but she'd always driven him to distraction.

"Blake, why so far—"

"I want you back here, Wren. You have a new computer and telephone. All the equipment and software you'll need to collect and analyze data. You'll get lots of work done—with no disturbances." No disturbances to me at the opposite end of the suite, he added silently.

"But I thought I'd be out in the field. That's what I'm good at. You haven't really seen me work, but the Nestlings account will need—"

"You don't have the Nestlings account yet, Wren." He watched the excitement in her eyes dim briefly and he felt like a heel.

"But I—"

"You have an idea, Wren, and one of the first things you'll learn in this business is that it takes a lot more than an idea to win a client."

As her boss, it was his responsibility to keep her at least partially grounded in reality. He watched the all-too-familiar beginnings of determination alter the set of her mouth.

"Blake, I—"

"The Nestlings proposal will be a good beginner's exercise for you, Wren."

And back here in the corner, her untempered optimism wouldn't run amuck and stir up the whole office. She would have to learn that what she'd been able to accomplish on the telephone wouldn't automatically work in person.

"You know where the supplies are. If you have any questions, I'll be in my office. Just let me know when you think you're ready with that proposal."

"But I already—"

Before she could manage another protest, before she could hook him with the stubbornness that clearly tilted her faintly dimpled chin, he turned and strode away.

Halfway across the room, he slowed to a stop, searching the desktops. Spotting a computer print-out, he picked it up, but instead of studying it, he found himself looking back at Wren against his will. He muttered an oath. She'd managed to distract him from his purpose—again.

She had laid her briefcase on the desk and was slowly circling her new space, examining everything like an eager puppy sniffing out new terrain. For a moment, she stood pondering the bare walls that formed her little niche.

Curious, he watched her pop open the briefcase and extract a yellow pad and pen. Writing with one hand, she pulled out the desk chair with the other and dropped into it. She raised the pen, studied what she'd written, then stabbed a sharp period onto the page. Turning back to the briefcase, she pulled out a folder and opened it.

Then she smiled. A soft smile that made her look as if she guarded a secret. He knew without thinking that the secret had to do with babies... a secret that made him all too aware of his thirty-one single years.

Hastily he returned the data to the desk in front of him and headed for the door. Burying his hands in his pockets, he encountered his keys. The touch scattered emotions through him like buckshot, driving him back to the solitude of his office.

Out of habit, he fingered the largest key, the one he'd acquired when he'd been with the accounting firm in St. Louis. Just a silly souvenir of his nephew Jack's magic act, but the key served Blake's purpose. He *wanted* it to remind him of that evening five years ago, the night the woman he'd hoped to marry had fallen in love... with someone else. Whatever had existed between him and Cathleen Kohlmann had been an illusion. Just like Jack's magic.

Love was an illusion. If ever, for a moment, he forgot, he had the key to remind him. His only reality was work, the one thing he would commit his life to now. And although he'd denied it to Wren, the truth was, he was too much like his father in that.

Blake surveyed the neatly stacked projects on his desk that needed his attention. For once, in spite of what was admittedly a distorted work ethic, the prospect of digging in left him agitated. He strode to the windows and stared out.

Snow. A fresh fall of snow on the mountains! Hell, he hadn't been up to the slopes yet this year, and January was already half over.

He needed a break. Maybe he'd go this afternoon. Take Sunday...Monday, too. Head up to ski with Kyle Kramer.

Wren's damned baby idea could wait till Tuesday. He could say no on Tuesday just as well as today.

Standing in the doorway of his office, Wren watched Blake talk into the phone on the credenza behind his desk. She never tired of looking at him, this golden man whose broad shoulders rippled beneath the soft weave of his dove-gray sweater.

She might have stood there indefinitely, except that when he put down the receiver and shoved a drawer closed, it dawned on her what he might be doing.

He stood and reached for his black suede jacket hanging on the coat tree in the corner.

"Blake, what are you doing?"

"I'm putting on my jacket. It's what people do when it's cold outside."

She thought she detected a glimmer of guilt, but it was hard to tell through that patronizing big-brother attitude.

"You're *leaving?* You can't leave."

"Oh?"

One dark gold eyebrow hitched northward, causing her breath to catch. "You can't leave unless you're coming right back."

His other brow rose to align with the first in exaggerated inquiry. She plunged on. "I have the Nestlings proposal ready, and I need your approval to get started on it."

"You have it done *already?*" He eyed her suspiciously, then appeared to make a decision. "If it's a good proposal, it'll be good tomorrow. And Tuesday—which is when I'll be back. That'll give you a chance to polish it."

"Tuesday?" Now what was she going to do? "Blake, you can't...."

"I can't?"

He sounded supremely annoyed, but this time she was sure she heard a hint of curiosity, too.

"I mean, I only need a few minutes. Here." She hurried forward to snatch his jacket from his hands, then gestured to his chair. "Just sit down. I promise I won't take long."

"Wr-en."

"Please, Blake, this is important." She dragged the side chair into the aisle to form a barricade and positioned herself in it like an anchor. This was no time for subtlety.

He scowled back at her, but at last he sat down. "Five minutes."

"Right."

Removing her summary from the file, she laid the folder on his desk. "Okay," she said, testing her voice for shakiness. "Nestlings consists of two retail stores that sell merchandise for the expectant mother during pregnancy. Also, items for mom and baby through the first year after birth."

She was talking too fast, she knew, but he had to hear it all before he bolted.

"Their main store is in Cherry Creek Mall, but in spite of the location, their sales are disappointing. My friend told her dad, Mr. Mason—he's the owner—that their merchandise isn't practical enough. We're supposed to find out what kinds of stuff new mothers want." Hearing herself chattering, she stopped.

Blake pounced like a cougar about to finish off a cricket. "They want product-development data? Wren, the big companies have that research all wrapped up." He pushed his chair back.

"Then why can't my friend find power-suit maternity clothes at a reasonable price?"

"What?"

Blake actually looked unsettled. Wren smothered a smile. What did a man who was married to his business know about maternity clothes? "I think it's because the big companies aren't researching right. I think new mothers have lots of good ideas, but they don't have time for phone inquiries and mail-in questionnaires."

Blake's chin dipped, and he scrutinized her from the top of his eyes. "So you, Wren March, a brand-new and, I might add, very inexperienced researcher, think you can do better than the big, deep-pocket companies?"

She wasn't sure he expected an answer, but she nodded enthusiastically, her heartbeat quickening.

"Just how do you propose to do that?"

"I'll ask the women. In person." It was exactly the kind of risk he might be willing to take.

He studied her with a withering glare. Finally he reached for the Nestlings file. His frown still set in concrete, he turned the pages slowly, scanning, thumb and forefinger abrading his jaw. In the silence, she could hear the whispery rasp. He read on and his hand stilled.

She had all but run out of breath when he finally looked up. "This is an expensive way to research, Wren. It could cost Nestlings a bundle."

He hadn't closed the file! She grasped the arms of the chair and slid forward. "I think I can sell Mr. Mason on the ideas." In the endless interval that followed, she was sure he would hear her heart pounding.

Blake shoved his chair back. "All right, Wren. Set up a meeting for Tuesday and leave the proposal with me. I'll look it over while I'm gone so I can come up with how we'll present."

Air slid from her lungs like a deflating balloon. "I can't, Blake."

"You can't what?"

"I can't set up a meeting for Tuesday. I've already set one up for Monday." She ignored what sounded like a growl. "Mr. Mason and his board will be here at nine. And his daughter, the one I graduated with, she's on the board. She requested that I make the presentation."

Blake's eyes darkened. With precise movements, he closed the file, then rose and hovered over her. Reaching down, he lifted his jacket from her knees.

Wren pushed to her feet, only to find herself staring into the soft gray of his sweater. She could detect the faint scent of something spicy on his skin and feel the warmth emanating from him. Without looking, she could sense the aggravation on his face, and she knew she had to stand her ground.

"Blake, I can do a good job. You have to let me do my own work sometime, you know. You have to let me prove myself." Though she stood very still, her breathy voice sounded as if she'd been running.

She compelled herself to look up then, past the stern set of his mouth to the fierce depths of his eyes. That turned out not to be such a good idea.

His scowl faltered. Tiny lines deepened at the corner of his eyes as he examined her, confusion taking shape out of the storm of his gaze. His eyes shifted, and she thought she felt something feather her mouth. Like the brush of a warm smooth thumb across her lower lip, sending a ribbon of heat coiling through her. Almost imperceptibly, he nodded.

Before she could stop him, he clasped her by the shoulders and turned her to the side. Grabbing the chair, he set it out of his path with a thump. The memory of his hands on her shoulders burned.

Wren fully expected him to depart with "Frankly, kid, I don't give a damn." Which would leave her with a whole lot to think about tomorrow...and the days and weeks that followed. Instead, he brushed by her, and she felt again the aura of his golden warmth.

He stopped in the doorway, jacket slung over his shoulder. In his other hand he twirled his keys. "Okay,

Wren. Monday morning. Nine o'clock. You make the presentation. This will be your probationary project."

Her heart took a flying leap. "Will you be here?"

"Of course. And, Wren ... ?"

"Yes?"

She watched in shock as his eyes swept over her. Inch by inch, she felt his gaze touch her—sliding from the wisps of flyaway hair that always escaped her ponytail, drifting along the faint curves of her sweatshirt, down the tight fit of her jeans, coming to an abrupt halt at her scruffy running shoes.

She could barely find voice to answer, but she managed to squeak out, "What?"

"Please dress appropriately."

Chapter Two

Blake shot off the elevator at the fifth floor and headed for the stairs. Throwing his camel topcoat over his arm, he took the last flight two steps at a time, grumbling all the way.

Sunday on the slopes with Kyle Kramer had turned out to be about as therapeutic as basic training in Siberia with a KGB interrogator. Which was probably why he'd overslept this morning. He *never* overslept.

He covered the length of the hall to his suite, then paused, one hand on the polished chrome latch, and glanced at his watch.

Eight-thirty. Damn. Almost an hour late, no coffee and that nagging sense of his life whirling out of kilter. Hell of a way to start a Monday morning with a potential new client.

If he was going to see a dry run of Wren's presentation before the Nestlings people arrived, he'd have to push it. Muttering another oath, he hauled the door open and strode through.

The rich aroma of coffee filled his nostrils, mingled with the scent of something warm from an oven. His stomach rumbled. No, caffeine would have to wait. He nodded to his secretary and cut through the telemarketing area.

In the workroom, the two men and two women who were his full-time staff greeted his arrival. Correction, he thought, testily. Four of his *five* full-time staff. At the sight of the empty desk chair in the corner, he stopped, fighting a flare of annoyance mixed with a touch of concern. It was an unaccountable reaction that faded almost unnoticed as he made note of the vase bursting with white daisies sitting on the desktop. Two large paintings, watercolors from the looks of them, filled the corner with vibrant light. All evidence pointing to Wren's early occupancy.

Good. He'd get his secretary to track her down. Send her to his office for a last-minute briefing.

Now for that cup of caffeine—to settle his uneasiness, because the weekend sure as hell hadn't. He never should have mentioned Wren's project to Kyle. Why should Kyle care what Wren looked like or if she could ski? Or if she was dating anyone, for crying out loud.

In the supply room, Blake poured an oversize mug of coffee, swallowing hard as the first steaming gulp seared all the way down his throat. Damn. He could still hear Kyle's laughter when he'd accused him of interest bordering on perversion. But after all Wren was still just a *kid*.

Blake hurried past the conference room, then skidded to a halt, setting the hot liquid in his cup sloshing dangerously. Backing up, he peered in.

Wren was there, her back to the door, talking to a blond woman not much taller than she and half a dozen men. Wren actually wore a suit—with a skirt, he noted—and her hair fell below her shoulders. She'd heeded his caution to dress appropriately. That offered at least some measure of promise for the morning.

The other woman's thick waist and shapeless dress suggested she was expecting—the daughter of Nestling's owner, no doubt, along with his other board members. If everyone was here, he wouldn't have time for a review with Wren. He didn't know what that promised.

The woman looked up and caught his eye, then spoke to Wren. On cue, everyone turned toward the door. Wren was the last to turn.

"Mr. Brockman. I've just been telling Trish and Mr. Mason about how you started your company."

Blake registered a fleeting impression of a bright red suit and shiny black heels. Then his gaze focused, like a close-up camera, on hair as dark and rich as the scent of his coffee. An abundance of soft sable curls framed her glowing face, and her eyes were just as dark and luminous, accented by the inquiring arch of her eyebrows. She tilted her head and smiled a welcome.

He hadn't felt it coming—an earthquake rarely announced its impact. He was totally unprepared for the shock that struck.

Was this Wren?

"I see you've found some coffee," she said, as if the room stood perfectly still. "We have muffins and fruit here, too. Please, come in and let me introduce you to everyone."

Still smiling, she beckoned, and he moved forward on a surface that seemed to tilt and sway.

"Mr. Brockman, this is Lisle Mason and his daughter, Trish Warren, and these are the other Nestlings."

Everyone laughed and stepped up to shake his hand, offering their names in turn. Blake went through the motions, impatient to be done so that he could look again at this woman who barely reached his chin, whose hundred or so pounds of subtle curves couldn't possibly create an earthly cataclysm. Was this Wren, the pipsqueak he'd been calling "kid" for years?

She looked up at him, and he saw something else he hadn't realized. Her eyes weren't brown. They were the color of sweet mocha liqueur. Her lips were faintly pink and incredibly, invitingly *full*. Lips meant to be kissed.

Another shock hit as he felt himself respond to her. Automatically he dug for the silver key he'd dropped into his suit coat pocket that morning. He had to get a grip.

What he was experiencing, what he *saw*, was nothing but illusion...a mirage created by cosmetics and hairstylists and orthodontists. Good God, she'd still been wearing braces on Saturday. Hadn't she?

"It's not nine o'clock," Wren said, "but everyone's here, so if you're ready, Mr. Brockman, we'll get started."

No, he wasn't ready...not at all, not for this...woman. Somewhere along the line, he'd missed her growing up. But no one else in the room seemed aware of that seismic revelation.

"Yes, of course." He laid his overcoat on the back of a chair and followed slowly behind the others to the conference table. Wren had already claimed the head chair, so he retreated to the far end and sat down.

Wren remained standing, and it occurred to him that until this morning he would have found that amusing. Now he wasn't sure what he felt, though it smacked suspiciously of respect.

"I'm so happy to welcome everyone to Brockman Incorporated," Wren began, "especially my good friend, Trish Warren." She paused to smile around the table, letting her gaze rest a moment on Blake.

In spite of his wariness, he couldn't help but absorb her warmth. He leaned back a little in the chair.

"By way of review," she continued, "when Trish learned she was expecting, she assumed everything she would need for her pregnancy, and for her baby, would be available through Nestlings. But as she has looked for particular products, she hasn't found them. Nor can the Nestlings buyers. That led her to. . ."

Blake had never noticed the silky confidence of Wren's voice, but it washed over him now, lulling him into a kind of soothing lethargy. He'd never noticed her hands, small hands—perfectly suited to her size— but with fingers surprisingly long and slender. Her nails were a natural pink, he observed with approval.

When she spoke, her gestures were subtle, made only for emphasis or persuasion. Feminine. Somehow he knew that her hands would have a gentle touch.

The thought created another aftershock that set him reaching for his coffee mug. He downed the last of the liquid in one gulp and grimaced at the cold dregs, a bitter reminder that he should be paying attention to the presentation.

"So I propose to do all of the research at the source," she continued. "We'll interview women at maternity shops, in baby departments, in maternity wards, at..."

Good Lord, she was laying it all out at once. The coffee mug clacked as he set it on the table. "Wren, I think—"

"Excuse me, Mr. Brockman," Trish Warren interrupted. "If you don't mind, we'd like to hear the entire proposal before any discussion."

If he didn't mind? Last week Aunt Ruby had given Wren her shares in his company. Overnight, Wren had grown up. So far this morning he'd managed to survive an earthquake *and* cold coffee. Why should he mind a client directing the sales presentation?

"Certainly." He waved a hand in the air and slouched back into the chair. Right away, he lost the battle to avoid looking at Wren.

He was glad to see she showed no signs of smugness. What he saw instead surprised him, a faint flash of relief that barely shimmered on the surface of the warming radiance she still projected.

She hesitated only a second. "We have to find a way to tap into women's creative ideas, to catch them when they're not harried and strapped for time. We have to go to settings where they can relax and think. *Then* we have to ask the right questions."

Against his will, Blake found himself enjoying her. Nestlings was a good learning experience for her, he had to admit. It would give her a chance to try her wings and him an opportunity to observe her. Professionally. He'd have to start thinking of her more professionally.

The only drawback to this experience was that Nestlings would turn her down. Her ideas were okay—pretty good, in fact—but too expensive for such a small firm. She wanted to do too much in the field.

But she had to learn. Nestlings was good practice, especially since she insisted on doing things her way. At least this was an account he wouldn't mind losing while she learned.

She was obviously ready for other projects, though. He could use her for...

Blake admired the way Wren moved as she talked, circling the oval table to deliver a folder of material to each person. He caught a glimpse of well-developed calves and slender ankles, making him reflect a moment on whether he'd ever seen her legs before. Suddenly he found himself remembering Kyle's questions. *Did* she ski?

Did she *date?*

He sat up straighter. Of course she did. Attractive young women dated. But that was of no concern to him.

As her employer, all he needed to know was that Wren wasn't a funny little chick anymore. As a smart employer, his only interest lay in making better use of an eager worker. As a hereditary workaholic, his only dates were with his mistress of a company.

"That about sums it up. Are there any questions?" Wren pulled out her chair and sat down, resisting an urge to check the weather in Blake's eyes. Beneath the conference table, her legs shook as if someone were jackhammering the floor.

She'd known she could handle the Nestlings presentation. She was pretty sure she could have handled the board of directors of *Big Blue* if she'd had to. But she knew just as well that if she got caught in Blake's gaze and saw clouds gathering there, he would cause serious damage to her dreams.

Gathering her determination, she looked at him for the first time since she'd started talking. "Mr. Brockman, you had something to add?"

He studied the pages of the folder in front of him, his downturned face frustrating her from reading the azure shading of his eyes, the degree of tightening in his jaw. He wasn't even toying with the silver key that seemed to be his version of a worry stone.

The shush of turning pages sliced through the room's silence. When he looked up, his eyes were still shadowed. "Thank you, Wren. I think you've covered everything."

Blake smiled the cordial business-owner's smile that turned his eyes opaque and told her absolutely nothing. She wished he would at least thunder a little. If they were going to be partners, he simply had to communicate better.

Lisle Mason cleared his throat. "Ms. March? I have some questions."

"Of course, Mr. Mason." Good grief, she'd all but forgotten the Nestlings people.

Lisle Mason raised several issues, and she started with the first, detailing her proposed procedures, but her awareness stayed tuned to Blake.

She saw his eyes stray to the gold bird's-nest pin, a thirteenth-birthday gift from her dad, on the lapel of her suit. She wondered if Blake even noticed she'd dressed up.

"... so we'll try to cover at least two sites a week," she answered Mr. Mason.

"I see. Ms. March, I wonder if you would consider contracting the project on a site-by-site basis until we determine just how successful this approach will be."

"Mr. Mason, I think that's..." Wren caught herself just in time, "... something Mr. Brockman will have to answer."

Blake stretched out of the chair and began to pace. It dawned on her that he'd been more interested in her proposal than she'd thought. He always paced when he was working on a problem.

Unfortunately, Lisle Mason had given Blake the perfect out. He'd already made it distressingly clear that the last thing he wanted his company to research was babies. All he had to decide was how to say no to Lisle's suggestion diplomatically.

"That's an approach we've never used before, Mr. Mason."

He was stalling, another of Blake's talents, the uncanny ability to turn clients' objections around so they went away feeling they'd just invented bread—without suspecting that Blake had accomplished exactly what *he'd* intended.

But this time what Blake intended affected her.

"Mr. Brockman, maybe we should discuss this and get back to Mr. Mason later. I could crunch some numbers and—"

"I don't think that will be necessary, Wren. I've already made up my mind."

She waited, forcing herself not to squirm. Strands of tawny hair had fallen across Blake's forehead. She could almost hear his thoughts churning toward thunder.

For a moment, his gaze settled on her. His eyes were March-wind gray.

"Your first proposed site is the Nestlings shop itself?"

His question caught her off balance. "My first...? I mean, yes. The one at Cherry Creek Mall."

A taunting shiver crept up her neck. Why did he have to draw out the torture? Why didn't he just say no?

Blake pushed fingers back through his hair. "Mr. Mason, my answer to that kind of suggestion has always been no..."

Wren closed her eyes.

"...under normal circumstances," Blake continued. "But Wren's proposal lends itself to trying something different."

Her eyes flew open at the same time her heart leapt like a kite catching the wind.

"I'll tell you what," Blake said, still not looking at her. "We'll work up a figure for you. If it's acceptable, Wren can begin at Cherry Creek whenever you're ready."

Blake had agreed to Lisle Mason's suggestion! Wren was still in a state of shock—and elation—as she helped Trish Warren distribute questionnaires and pencils on the table they'd just set up along one side of the Nestlings shop.

"Wren, I think we should add one more place here," Trish suggested.

"You don't think it will block women from getting to the dressing rooms?"

"No, and I think we should have an extra place in case your boss comes by."

Wren repressed a twinge of anticipation and glanced at Trish, fully prepared for her teasing grin. She wasn't disappointed.

"I don't think he's coming, Trish. I didn't ask him."

"You didn't *ask* him?" Trish looked like a mother working up to a reprimand.

"Wren, could you come out here a minute and check the door-prize box?" a grandmotherly woman interrupted.

"You bet." Wren jumped at the chance to get away from the scolding she knew was coming. "Trish, go ahead and add another place if you think it'll fit. But don't expect Blake to show."

He wouldn't, she knew. She'd been torn between wanting him there to share her first big assignment and wanting to accomplish it on her own. Ultimately, she had decided he'd be too much of a distraction.

This first research had to be a booming success. She would ask Blake to the later sites, which would contribute more toward her purposes anyhow.

Wren followed the woman she'd hired for part-time interviews to the front of the Nestlings shop where a blue box with a giant pink bow sat on a pedestal.

"Is this location okay?" the woman asked.

"Let's move it nearer the window. And how about some stuffed animals? Maybe even a couple holding the sign?"

She helped the woman rearrange the display, then stepped back to read the instructions on the placard. *Deposit The Coupon From Your Questionnaire Here For A Chance To Win A Complete Maternity Outfit.* Satisfied that the lettering was easy to read, she spun away. And almost collided with Jaime.

"Hey, Bird Woman, Ted and I need your expertise in the rug-rat room."

"Jaime, you look perfect!" Wren cocked her head to admire his mouse ears and the giant teddy bear tucked under his arm. She laughed. "I can't believe you actually volunteered for baby-sitting duty." She walked with him toward the small room in the back.

"Why not? You don't think an eligible and highly desirable bachelor likes kids? You don't like kids, maybe?"

She laughed again and tweaked his giant ear fondly. "I love kids. But I'm not making any proposals today, even if *you* love them, too."

Jaime was a good friend, but the only bachelor she was interested in was not, presently, what she would call eligible. All signs indicated that Blake needed some serious work in the kids department, too.

"Can't blame me for trying, Wren. But I'm a patient man. In the meantime, check me out and see if we're childproof."

Wren glanced around the small room, at the bright paintings on the walls and the wealth of toys spread all over the floor.

"This is fine. But you need to separate the toys into age groups. Put the little tykes at the far end and the bigger kids nearer the door. It'll save you a lot of headaches."

"Sounds like you have lots of younger brothers and sisters."

She shook her head no. "I was an only child, but I baby-sat a lot. Started when I was eleven."

She hardly thought about those days anymore. She'd loved the kids, many of them not much younger than herself. But she had especially loved the babies.

All those kids had been the family she and her dad missed. And they'd been a way for her to earn money, to make up for what her dad's handiwork around Antler hadn't brought in.

"Wren," Trish called from the front of the store. "There are women already waiting outside. They must have seen your ad. Get ready, 'cause it's ten o'clock, and we're opening the doors."

Trish's urgency tripped Wren's excitement. This was it. If all her planning and preparations worked, Mr. Mason would extend the contract, Brockman Incorporated would earn a substantial fee and she would begin the monumental task of moving the immovable Blake Brockman.

Chapter Three

Blake had no intention of going by the Nestlings shop. This was Wren's project, a project he hadn't wanted in the first place. He still wasn't sure what had made him accept Lisle Mason's suggestion. He was even less sure it had been wise.

The one thing he *did* know for certain was that Wren had to learn the business through experience. Besides, he had more important things to do on a Saturday than satisfy idle curiosity. So he buried himself in a multitude of small tasks, told himself he was much too busy to leave the office. Yet, in the end, he went simply because he couldn't stay away.

"Mr. Brockman!" Trish Warren spotted him standing outside Nestlings. "Thank goodness you're here. We could sure use your help." She took Blake's arm and tugged him through the entryway.

Blake decided quickly on the wisdom of yielding, partly because he could imagine the scene if he didn't:

one tall, very reluctant male being dragged into a maternity shop by one very short and obviously pregnant woman. But mostly he yielded because he couldn't believe what he was seeing.

"Where did all these pregnant women come from?"

Trish laughed. "I could tell you we're the results of Rocky Mountain highs, but this is going on all over the nation. Come on. We need another interviewer."

Trish led him to the side of the store where a cluster of women in various stages of roundness munched cookies while they waited in a line. The line extended to a table at which more women sat, talking to people he recognized—some of his part-time interviewers— and Wren, sitting at the far end.

The sight of her shouldn't have unsettled him, but it did. She still looked like the beautiful young woman who'd materialized in his conference room Monday morning. Gone were the familiar blue jeans and ponytail, and the rest of the week she continued to look like a corporate princess, even though he'd expected, at any time, to hear the clock strike twelve and see her dash from the office before her carriage turned back into in-line skates.

He was still waiting.

"Here." Trish shoved a stack of questionnaires and a fistful of pencils into his hands. "There's an empty place on the side by Wren. The questionnaire's self-explanatory. Ladies, whoever's next, follow this good-looking dude." Flashing Blake a grin, she sped away to the cash register.

At Trish's announcement, Wren looked up, and he saw the wide-eyed surprise he hadn't even known he'd anticipated. She mouthed the word "Hi," and her face brightened with a pleased smile. Blake folded himself into the chair around the corner of the table from her, wanting to turn and study this newly discovered butterfly up close.

"You said there was a baby boomlet," he murmured out of the side of his mouth. "This looks more like galloping contagion. I thought the economy was supposed to be tight." He couldn't stay away from her eyes, though he wished he had when he discovered a silvery twinkle in their dark depths.

"Going to a movie is expensive," she whispered, "but the pizza *delivery* business is great."

It took him a whole beat to catch her innuendo. He could feel heat creep up his neck at the same time he gave in to a reluctant grin. This was definitely not the little Wren he used to know.

On the other side of the table a large woman pulled out the metal folding chair to sit down. One glance and he jumped up to extend a hand to her. The woman had to be almost as tall as he, and as big-boned as any man, which wouldn't have brought him to his feet, except that she was the most pregnant woman he'd ever seen. She should have delivered twins at least a week ago, he was sure.

He must have looked alarmed, because she waved him away. "It's okay, lovey," she said, puffing, lowering herself into the chair. "I'm a big woman and I have big babies. But not for a month or so yet, so don't be worrying."

Should a woman this pregnant even be out on a snowy day?

The only help Wren offered was an amused smile and a small nod of encouragement. She nudged the questionnaires nearer. "I'll bet this lady has some good ideas to share."

"Right." An inexcusable lapse of mettle on his part. He'd researched Navy Seals and prison inmates, for crying out loud. A few expectant women shouldn't shake his moorings. Especially when Wren was having no trouble at all.

Concentrating on the woman's freckled face, he covered the demographic items on the questionnaire. This was her third pregnancy, she told him, and she *was* expecting twins. She and her husband were both in their latter thirties.

"Isn't that sort of unusual?" Blake asked.

"You mean twins, or our ages? Or both?" She laughed, obviously enjoying his interest. "Most of my pregnant friends are older than I am."

Wren leaned close. "Makes you feel downright damp behind the ears, doesn't it?"

"In your case, I'd say damp in the..." Blake stopped, caught in the faint sweet scent of her perfume and a fleeting image of wildflowers. He'd been going to tease her about diapers. She was hardly more than a kid, but lately he couldn't seem to keep that in mind.

"In my case, Blake?"

Wren's smile was thoroughly wicked, something else totally new. Something he wasn't prepared to deal with. Retreating, he answered, "In *my* case, I have the right to remain silent...I have the right..."

Wren laughed, that quick sparkling burst of surprise that had always annoyed him. Except that today it struck an answering laughter in him that was also new. And exhilarating.

Still smiling, he returned to the questionnaire. "Are there any items of maternity clothing you'd like to see made available?" he read.

The woman rested her hands on the shelf of her roundness. "That's why I came in. Not all of us women are petite little things like this one." She gestured to Wren. "I have to buy my maternity clothes at big women's stores. What women my size need is an extender."

"An extender?" Blake ventured, suddenly wary of the radical new direction her answer seemed to have taken and about how he would handle it.

"Like a rubber band, only nonbreakable. Not all those big clothes have elastic waistbands, you know. We need something that'll hook into a buttonhole and slip around the button, so when the waists get too small, we don't have to go buy something else."

"I see." He exhaled slowly while he wrote her answer, almost certain that the warmth he felt down his neck came from Wren watching. "Anything else?" he asked reluctantly.

"I don't understand why no one has come out with a shirt with flap pockets." The woman beamed.

Using just a little imagination, Blake was pretty sure this explanation would be even more vivid than the last. He risked a glance at Wren. She was busy writing, but he could see amusement curling the corners of her full mouth.

For a brief crazy moment, he wanted to slip a finger under her chin and nudge gently to challenge whatever humor he found in those dark dancing eyes. The very idea loosed a glow of heat that traveled much lower than his neck.

Unwillingly, he asked, "Could you...elaborate?"

"For nursing, lovey."

Just as he'd feared. To his dismay, the woman gestured toward her ample bosom.

"I've tried those tops with the overlays and openings and such, but trying to get everything unsnapped and unflapped is a trick for Mrs. Houdini herself. Give me pockets. Double pockets, *big fake* pockets that I could lift *up,* like so..." She moved her hands to demonstrate, and Blake felt his heat detonate into rampant embarrassment.

"They'd have to invent something besides zippers or Velcro so it wouldn't scratch the baby," the woman said, continuing to illustrate with her hands.

Blake concentrated on writing furiously.

"I think that's a marvelous idea."

He could hear the laughter in Wren's voice. "Excellent idea," he agreed, grateful for his task as scribe."I've got it. That's all the questions for today."

Despite her protests, the woman let him help her up from the chair. He watched her bulky departure with a mixture of embarrassment and respect. Wren's eyes glowed with a delight that did little to cool his chagrin.

"You may have just gotten the best suggestion we've had all day," she said. "There's a prize, you know."

"Prize?"

"Nestlings is giving a gift certificate to the interviewer who gets the most viable product suggestion."

"Since I don't see maternity clothes in my future, I think I'll withdraw from the competition."

Blake actually saw her pupils contract, making her look both vulnerable and wary. Her retort was a pulse beat too long in coming.

"That's good, because they're definitely not your style." Her easy camaraderie had disappeared. "Also, the other interviewers will appreciate it."

She slid the questionnaire she'd just completed to the bottom of the pile. "I . . . appreciate your helping, too," she said, a little less stiffly. "I never imagined we'd have such a turnout."

Nor had Blake imagined that Wren's words, in that quiet voice, with just a catch of hesitation, could cause the earth to shift again. But it did; only this time it was more subtle, more elusive. And because of that, more dangerous.

Not a national disaster. More of a personal threat, like a house shifting with time, causing a chink in the walls, a crack through which feelings could creep. Feelings he couldn't name. He only knew that when the fun faded from her eyes, when he heard that rare uncertainty in her voice, something stirred inside him, something he'd put away a long time ago.

Dragging his gaze from her unreadable face, he squared his own stack of papers on the table. "I like to help inexperienced employees." The words sounded harsher than he'd intended and started a rush of guilt, because the truth was he hadn't planned to help at all.

Damn.

Somehow Wren had managed to touch his feelings. But he was determined to ignore them. He couldn't let feelings entangle his life again.

"At this rate, I won't be inexperienced for long." Wren made a show of counting the women still waiting to be interviewed. Beckoning to the next in line, she tapped her collection of papers on the tabletop, creating a flurry of noise and activity to cover her spiraling spirits.

She'd been so flustered to see Blake here, too eager to see the flash of his smile and hear his slow laughter. She'd pushed him and teased him until he'd backed away, bristling like a lion annoyed by a playful cub.

But he was always quick to recover. She watched him welcome another woman with that spell-casting smile and help her sit. The woman laughed shyly, a flush coloring her cheeks, a reaction Wren had witnessed more times than she could count.

But it wasn't Blake's smile that got to her, nor his polished ruggedness and easy charm that made him so overpowering. It was his force, his drive. His need. She wondered if other women saw it—the passion that drove him. Like his father, he put work before everything.

Terrible misdirected passion. That thought always generated more than a girlish blush in her. As usual, it evoked a spreading warmth that made her shift in her chair.

"Just because I showed up doesn't mean it's break time for the neophyte," Blake murmured. "Don't leave now, because I just saw Ruby come in. Probably checking on the new shareholder."

"Ruby's here?" Wren spotted her inspecting nursery lamps near the front of the store. The sight of Blake's aunt made her smile. Hard to miss a pixie-faced white-haired woman in a bright purple snowsuit.

She should have known Ruby would show up at her first field activity, especially since Blake and his company ranked right up there at the top of her list of things to keep her eye on.

Thanks to Ruby, Blake's company was partly hers now, too, a move, she suspected, that represented several more of Ruby's favorite projects—namely *Wren* . . . and matchmaking.

Wren had learned early on that it didn't do any good to discourage Ruby from her campaigns. At least she was a well-intentioned ally, and Wren knew how fortunate she was to have her. Ruby was the closest she'd come to having a real mother.

Three interviews later, her suspicions grew when she discovered Ruby beaming at her from the front of the line.

"I'm just visiting, dear," she said. "Chatting with this nice young lady and Ryan here." She smiled at a woman with short black hair wearing a white sweat suit. Appliquéd across the fullness of her round middle, in bright red and green letters, was the word *Watermelon.*

Wren laughed out loud.

Small hands crept out on either side of the woman's thighs and grasped her soft pants tightly. A head of blond hair slipped into view at just the height of her "watermelon," and two light blue eyes followed, full of watchfulness. Abruptly the little head ducked out of sight.

Wren barely heard Blake's quiet chuckle. No way was she going to look at him and send him vamoosing back to his lair, but the sound cheered her. Even if he denied the likelihood of maternity clothes in his future, he wasn't totally immune to the antics of a toddler.

The tousled head of sunshine reappeared from behind his mother's legs, and sparkling eyes zeroed in on Blake. Darn it, this wasn't something she could resist watching for long. She turned just in time to see Blake squinch his eyes closed in a funny face.

A giggle erupted from behind the woman's back, captivating laughter that made Wren fairly bubbly herself. She'd never seen Blake play. Her plan showed signs of beginning to work.

"Hang on, Ryan," the watermelon mother said. "We have to move forward now. Here we go...choo choo choo."

Her progress was slow, hampered by the boy's tight grip, but she didn't seem to mind. She aimed her round middle toward the chair in front of Wren and chugged forward with an apologetic smile. Ruby chugged alongside, curled down near the little boy, repeating, "I think I can, I think I can..."

Wren laughed again, her mood lifting by notches. Ruby had no inhibitions when it came to kids. She'd been the same with Wren from the day she'd come to live with her. Except that instead of stories about a train that could, Ruby had told her, over and over, about a young *girl* who could. Ruby never let her stop believing it.

"Toot, toot." The towheaded child peeked out again with two plump little fingers poked into the corners of his mouth. A small pink tongue crept into view.

Blake tilted his head to one side and lowered one eyelid in a broad wink, which drew another tummy-tickling giggle.

"I'll interview this one, Wren," Blake announced.

In a million years, she would never have said no. "Be my guest," she murmured. She knew better than to interfere when magic was at work.

"Okay, Ryan, time to put the train in the station. Thanks for the company," the watermelon mother said to Ruby. "And the advice. Say goodbye to the train lady, Ryan."

The woman settled into the chair in front of Blake. Two small hands appeared on her shoulders and a small voice piped up from behind the chair. "Bye-bye, Gam-maw."

"Oh, honey, she's not a grandma," his mother said, looking apologetic. She hugged him close, letting him hide his face on her shoulder.

"Now, Mom..." Blake's voice chastised warmly, "I think Ryan knows Grandma material when he sees it."

Wren's heart did a little flip and turned completely upside down. All around her, she saw the melting in every woman's eyes. Any second she expected to hear a collective "Awww."

Ruby shot her a thumbs-up, blew a kiss to Ryan and departed, leaving Wren humming inside. Little Ryan had coaxed out a clown with a great big heart. She'd seen Blake's face, and she'd suspected it all along. Somewhere inside Blake was a playfulness and a cherishing that he didn't even suspect. And somewhere inside him, she knew with all her heart, there was love, as well.

"Hey, big guy, what are you doing out here?" Jaime Sandoval stooped to talk to the little blond kid.

"I didn't know you were working on this project, Jaime." Blake eyed the big black ears clasped to the top of Jaime's head and the black animal nose attached over his own.

"Mr. Brockman." Jaime rose and snatched off the nose, making the round ears waggle. "I'm not. Not

officially, anyhow. I offered to help Wren with the
nursery. Gratis.''

Blake couldn't miss the wink Jaime flashed Wren.
His good humor slipped.

"I came to ask what you're doing for dinner, Wren,
but it looks like I have an escapee here." Jaime ruffled Ryan's corn-silk hair.

So this was one of the boys Wren dated, Blake reflected, though "boy" was hardly appropriate. Early
twenties, he'd guess—old enough to be called a man,
floppy ears and black nose notwithstanding. Young
enough to make Blake feel almost historical . . . and as
grumpy as the grim portraits in the history books.

"I don't know about dinner yet, Jaime," Wren answered. "If you have kids to watch, maybe I should
bring something to *you*. How's it going anyhow?"

"Great. You should come back and see. I might
even let you hold one of my babies." Jaime's smile
held more than simple regard.

Blake understood the underlying enticement for
Wren in Jaime's words and was surprised that he did.

"Wren's eating with me." The declaration surprised him even more. "I want her to give me an eval-
uation of the day's activities," he added. "We'll bring
something back for you, if you'd like." He hated
sounding so patronizing.

"Yes...of course we'll bring you something," Wren
echoed. "A hamburger okay?"

Almost his very words, yet Wren spoke with such
appeal. Maybe Jaime was someone special. Blake's
mood continued to drop.

"Sure." Jaime replaced the black nose slowly, the
gesture almost an act of challenge, before he knelt

down to Ryan again. "What do you say, big guy? Want to come play with all the toys?"

Ryan shook his head and buried his face in his mother's shoulder.

"Do you mind if he stays here?" his mother asked Blake. "He's having some separation anxiety. He won't be any trouble."

"You can stay right here, Ryan," Blake reassured him. Ryan's little shoulders wiggled, but his face stayed hidden.

"Guess I'd better get back to the kids." Jaime touched three fingers to his mouse ear and looked directly at Blake. "Mr. Brockman."

Blake barely nodded. Jaime had just aged him a full decade with that simple salute. The only consolation was that he hadn't called him Colonel.

What would it take to shake off this sudden attack of geriatrics? Blake wondered, to coax Ryan out again and recapture the play? What would it take to hear that kind of appeal in Wren's voice? He was sure as hell plagued with a lot of unexpected—and unacceptable—reactions today.

"You wanted to ask some questions?" Ryan's mother prompted.

"Yes." Blake tried to shake off his malaise. He never should have left the office. He should have buried that idle curiosity in the same faraway place he kept other feelings.

The woman answered each question thoughtfully, and as Blake bent to write, Ryan's bright blue eyes peeped out at him again.

Such a shy modkin. This little guy looked as if he could use a steady application of Aunt Ruby's "I think I can" philosophy. Couldn't everyone? Blake thought wryly, himself included.

"How many other children do you have at home?"

The woman slid an arm around Ryan's compact little body. Wistfulness crept into her eyes. "This is my first pregnancy."

Puzzled, Blake tipped his head toward Ryan. "What about..."

The woman nodded. "Foster care. We probably won't be able to... continue after the baby comes." The sudden brightness in her eyes looked like tears.

"I'm sorry," he managed to say. He was suddenly numb with anger. This little ragamuffin, this kid whose hair was as blond as Blake's had once been, whose sturdy little body could well grow long and lean just as his finally had, this child didn't live with his family.

Why?

Blake couldn't stop more questions from coming. Was it because he had a mother who'd almost finished raising the one daughter she'd planned on and was devoting her life to a new husband? Was it because he had a father whose love for his wife was surpassed only by his love for his career in the Marines?

People like that didn't want an unplanned towheaded boy-child to drag from base to base, assignment to assignment. People like that used foster-care homes to shove their kids off on. Or, if the kid was lucky, a loving Aunt Ruby.

People like that should never have kids.

Blake stood. "Let's see if we can find a lollipop for Ryan." Digging into his pocket, he found the shiny silver key. He scraped his thumb roughly across its square bits, then passed behind Wren, careful not to

brush against her, all too aware of her upturned face
and the worried questions in her eyes.

As a research analyst, he brooded, Wren would have
to learn that some questions should never be answered.

Chapter Four

Wren uncrossed her legs, then recrossed them. She tugged her short black skirt toward her knees. Automatically, she set the toe of her shiny black pump tapping the air, in time with her fingers drumming on the padded chair arm.

"You can stop fidgeting, Wren. I'm almost done. I hope you have a report for me." Blake continued signing the papers on his desk.

"A full report." And a check for five million dollars, she was tempted to add, just to see if he really was listening. Ever since Saturday, he'd been so submerged in work, she'd wondered if he'd ever surface for air.

"Good." He glanced up, his expression shifting from distant to a brief glimmer of surprise, as if he'd just discovered her there. The glimmer was followed by a definite darkening.

Unfortunately, his appearance suggested that Monday afternoon offered no improvement over his sudden bad turn of weather late Saturday...which accounted for her being as restless as a willow before a storm. Blake's white collar stood open, the knot of his neatly patterned tie loosened by an impatient tug. His suit jacket had been banished to the coat tree, and he'd rolled his shirtsleeves back from taut muscular forearms. Everything about him confirmed just how staunchly he'd dug back into his own work.

"There." The rasp of pen on paper pierced the silence, sending a shiver skittering down her spine. He stabbed the pen into its marble holder, scooped up the pile of papers, shook the corners square in a furor of efficiency and laid the pile near the edge of the desk.

He'd exhausted all his reasons to evade her.

Clearing his throat with a muffled growl, he leaned back. His glacier-blue eyes met hers. "Okay, Wren. I'm ready."

Her heart lurched. A bolt of lightning might just as well have zapped right down the coat tree behind him, because it couldn't have unsettled her more. Blake looked about as grim as an arctic explorer, which was a big improvement over the chilling mood that had engulfed him on Saturday. And all because of Ryan.

A foster child—who would have guessed?—an unexpected circumstance that must have reminded Blake of his own upbringing. Ruby had alluded to it, but Wren hadn't realized how deep Blake's resentment toward his parents still ran.

If only she'd been able to talk to him. If only they hadn't gotten so busy at the Nestlings Shop that they couldn't leave for the dinner Blake had suggested.

"*Wr-en.* The report?"

She breathed in sharply, felt her pulse kick into an erratic dance of dread and excitement. She was never ready when Blake looked so overpowering. He'd glower, and a rush of possibilities would overcome her. She had to make him see that his passion should be for living, not buried in the past. Or directed at the bottom line.

"The obstetric clinic this morning?" he prompted, sounding more patronizing and older-brotherish than ever.

"Blake, you can't imagine how well it went." She leaned forward, determined to break through the ice. "The doctors were—" catching the Nestlings folder before it slid from her lap, she scooted to the edge of the chair "—the doctors were full of ideas. And competitive. They were funny."

"Funny?" The lines between his brows deepened as he squinted at her.

She managed a smile in spite of her still-erratic heartbeat. "I wish you could have heard them. They were falling all over each other to come up with the best suggestion."

"Did they have any good ideas?"

She hesitated, heat touching her cheeks as she recalled the doctors' more intimate suggestions regarding the problems of nursing. She grasped at something less physical. "How about a Cracker Vacker?"

Blake's stony rock-man facade wavered, and she knew she'd caught his interest with the name. He would never notice the warmth in her cheeks.

"Would you care to elaborate?" His brow hitched the usual half notch she loved, exposing his reluctant curiosity.

"A miniature vacuum sweeper. Small enough to fit in a diaper bag along with everything else." At Blake's blank expression, she laughed. "They said the expectant mothers come in with a lot of 'crumby' kids. They want them to sweep up the trail of cracker crumbs their little ones leave."

For a fleeting moment, an elusive smile puckered the corners of his mouth, that endearing humor that hovered beneath his intensity, so often showing up just in time to catch her off guard. His eyes warmed to the color of mountain columbines.

"Doesn't sound very doctorly. Didn't they have any medical suggestions?"

Again she stalled, half amused, half sympathetic. Blake hadn't proven very stalwart in the face of some of the women's notions on Saturday. How would he handle the pragmatic ideas of men who spent the wee morning hours up to their elbows delivering babies?

"One doctor said if Nestlings could devise a formula to eliminate stretch marks, they could patent it and retire as millionaires," she hazarded.

Blake's face remained carefully passive as he considered the proposal, though she could tell it cost him some effort.

He nodded slowly. "He's right, of course, but I'm sure the big medical companies are working on that. What else?"

Come on, Blake, she wanted to coax. *You're not like the Colonel. Loosen up.* The temptation to prod was more than she could resist. "How about a Bellybutton Button?"

This time, both of Blake's eyebrows shot up, rewarding her with the flash of amazement she'd been poking around for. She couldn't help grinning at his loss of equanimity.

"I had to ask, too," she assured him. "You've heard of innies and outies?"

Blake took refuge in a frown, which only served to increase her delight. He nodded warily.

"The doctors explained that when some moms' tummies get very large, their outies show through their clothes. The mothers want a product that would give them a smooth look."

"Oh." Blake's frown relaxed. "I do hope Nestlings finds that useful information." His voice had colored with wry humor, and his eyes eased toward another smile.

"They especially liked that one." She couldn't resist one more nudge. "And someone in your future may be grateful for their solution, you never know."

"I *do* know."

His answer was too abrupt, his tone suddenly harsh, but it was his certainty that struck with the force of a winter wind, pressing her back into her chair. Fighting off a chill, she watched him launch himself and move to the windows.

For what seemed an eternity, he stood staring out, silhouetted against the gathering twilight. When he spoke, he was the businessman again. "Looks like another storm. Let's finish this up so you can get out of here before it starts snowing."

"Okay," she answered quietly. She'd pushed him too hard again, ruffled the lion's mane. "I dropped this morning's questionnaires off to Mr. Mason at noon. He seemed satisfied. It's all in the file here, along with the results from Saturday." She laid the folder on his desk.

She knew she should get up and turn on the lights, but the thought of the harsh brightness flooding the small office held her still. Better to keep her distress hidden in the early-evening shadows that had crept in to envelop them.

Blake picked up the file and returned to the windows, putting distance between them, she was sure. Trying to move Blake was risky business at best, an exercise that seemed to involve two halting steps forward followed by a heart-wrenching slide back.

She'd vowed to find a way to reach this man, to draw him out of his guarded fortress. But so far what she'd put him in touch with had only managed to drive him further away. Maybe her whole idea was a terribly misguided mistake.

"I'll be damned. Look at this."

Blake turned toward her as he spoke, but the darkening sky behind him cast his face in planes of gray. She couldn't read his expression, couldn't tell if she'd heard what sounded incredibly like respect.

He held up a slender piece of paper. "Your first fee earnings. A handsome check, too. You should be proud of this, Wren." He slipped the check back into the folder. "Saturday was a good job," he added gruffly.

A good job. The words didn't surprise her. Blake was always generous with praise for his employees. It was the way he said them that deepened her concern. As if, this time, the commendation came hard.

Back to square one. One step at a time. If you don't like the weather, wait and it will change. Rapidly she ticked off all the clichés she could think of to keep her spirits up. Clearly, she'd be wise to concentrate on winning Blake's business approval. She'd be best off working on becoming his business partner, because he obviously wasn't ready to let her reach his heart.

Blake rifled through the rest of the file, stopping at the packet of light blue pages Wren had designed as the Nestlings contract. "When will Lisle Mason let us know if they'll go ahead with the next activity?"

"He signed for the exercise class while I was at his office this morning." The excitement that had charged Wren's voice seemed to have evaporated.

With a jab of regret, Blake noticed she no longer sat on the edge of the chair. He flipped the contract pages to the terms for Phase Three. The new signatures were all there below the quoted fee—a rather substantial fee.

"You should have announced your conquest sooner." He managed to keep his voice even, to cover the jumble of feelings her subdued answer stirred.

"I knew you'd find it in the file. I...wanted to save it for last."

She'd intended it as a surprise, and he'd spoiled it. What was worse, the realization smarted.

Blake wasn't used to this, all these feelings showing up that he'd kept buried for years. He was like a walking hornets' nest—crawling with unwieldy emotions. At the least provocation, he was likely to sting. He'd just aptly demonstrated how much of a jerk he could be. Damn.

"I'm...pleased, Wren. I didn't expect Nestlings to go beyond one activity." He hadn't expected her ideas to reap such good results, either. Was such miserly praise all he could muster?

"I'm proud of you." He *was* proud of her, so why did he sound like a tight old Dutch uncle? The Nestling's account was a real coup, especially for a beginner. She was proving herself more competent with creative ideas than she'd ever been on the telephone. If she kept up this kind of growth, she'd become a substantial asset to his company.

"Thank you, Blake."

He allowed himself no more than a quick glance, but it was enough to take in her straight slender shoulders beneath the soft white blouse, the unyielding determination in that too-familiar tilt of her dimpled chin. Enough to provoke a startling impression of creamy silk over seductively sculpted steel. He muttered a silent curse.

In all the time little Wren had been around, she'd put up with his driven ways. She'd ignored him and badgered him and teased him endlessly. She'd been the only one—the *only* one—who'd risked teasing him. She'd never let him intimidate her.

And he had liked that. He'd never realized how much—how much he relied on it—until now. Now that he'd thundered her into withdrawal.

"Blake, if I can count on you for the next project, I could show a more profitable bottom line."

He watched her inch forward a bit on the chair. "How do you figure that?" he asked, careful to keep his tone mild.

"I wouldn't have to hire another temp, and I wouldn't have to pay *you* overtime." A hint of challenge sparked her dark eyes.

"You mean, you wouldn't pay me at *all*." He returned her dare, relieved to see her jousting again. Scrapping with Wren was far safer than dealing with what he no longer could deny. She wasn't *little* Wren anymore. Every time he saw her, every time he thought of her, his body made him distressingly aware that she'd grown up.

He didn't know how to handle that. He kept getting lost in the scent of wildflowers that drifted with her. She captivated him with the delicate blush that brightened her cheeks when she teased. He was tortured by glimpses of smooth slender thigh when she fidgeted in her chair. What was a man to do when such feelings threatened to swamp him?

"You were the one who told me the business owner is the last to get paid," she shot back. "I noticed you didn't turn in your time for Saturday."

Why did he hear bewitchment when all she meant was to kid? "I was there to observe," he demurred.

"You didn't look like you particularly liked what you saw. Was it Jaime's ears? Or all those pregnant women?"

She was looking downright wicked again, and even as he overheated, he discovered he was glad.

"Or was it that little kid Ryan?" she added, her voice suddenly serious.

The question jarred him, but this time he managed to smother an outburst. Wren was uncanny. She was far too young, much too innocent to home in on him so unerringly.

"I guess I just don't relate to the idea of families and children."

That was probably the understatement of the decade. How could he relate to family when the only one he'd ever known had given him away to someone else's care? How could he relate to children when growing up without a father around didn't teach him that?

But he had learned self-control, which was all he needed.

"What about you, Wren? You seemed comfortable with the mothers and their kids." As soon as he gave voice to the question, he wished he hadn't. He didn't want the conversation to continue in that direction.

She hesitated. "I like kids," she said, each word coming slowly, as if she weren't sure she wanted to say them. "I used to baby-sit a lot after...my mother left."

The thought seemed to propel her from the chair. For once their roles were reversed as he watched her pace.

"I love babies," she said with more confidence, "and toddlers." She paused. "I guess the truth is I like them all." She stood still, gazing into some memory, her lovely profile clearly defined in the dusk that filled his office. When she moved again, it was with conviction.

"And I want at least four of my own, in a big, two-story house full of baseball mitts and tap dance shoes and bicycles and miniature cars and video games and wet towels and Cheerios and—"

"Wren...?"

She snapped to a stop at his solemn inquiry, her face open with astonishment. If he hadn't spoken, she'd likely have charged right into him, which he realized, too late, would have been far less dangerous than where she stopped, just a few tantalizing inches away. She stared at him, her pupils as large as a doe's.

Against every ounce of his will, his gaze strayed to her lips. They were deliciously full, dusky pink...and open in mute surprise. He knew then that he wanted to kiss her, that he'd wanted to for a long time. Hell, he wanted to sweep her up and carry her off and...

"Whoa!" He said the word with as much humor as he could summon, given that his hands shook from not reaching for her, that his body ached from not having her pressed against him.

"Hold on, Wren. I'll get the lights." He eased around, taking care not to touch her, because he knew she would send currents of electricity zinging through him. Then he would have to act on what he saw in her eyes.

She wanted him to kiss *her*.

"There."

Bright light flickered from the fluorescent tubes overhead and settled into a steady hum, driving away the intimacy that had crept in. Blake escaped to the safety of his desk chair. Wren looked out the windows.

"How can you want that, Wren?" He grasped at the domestic scene she'd been painting, realizing too late the more immediate implication of his question.

"What do you mean?"

When she turned, she was squinting, whether from the stark light or his unintended double entendre, he couldn't be sure. He wasn't certain of much at the moment, including the wisdom of pursuing her feelings further. But he couldn't shake the compulsion to know.

"I mean, how can you consider having children after what happened to you?"

She tilted her head, a frown of puzzlement slanting her brows. "Blake, just because my mother left doesn't mean *I* will. Or that I'll die, like Dad did." She paused, and he saw her eyes clear. "Kids don't have to grow up to be like their parents."

She might believe that, but she'd had fifteen years with a loving father and time with Ruby ever since. Dear Aunt Ruby, who was full of enough nurturing and love for the whole earth... and an extra planet or two. Ruby would be Wren's model of a mother.

"Of course. I'm sure you'll make a wonderful mother." Unlike him, she was prepared to be a parent.

For a moment, she looked as if she wanted to say more, but instead she turned back to stare out the windows. He knew, from uncountable working nights, that beyond the glass, a vast sparkling sea stretched to the feet of the mountains and splashed drops of light up their darkening slopes.

"Blake, it's beginning to snow pretty hard. I think I'd better go home."

"You're right." He forced back the impulse to move behind her, to slip his arms around her, to nestle his nose in the wildflower scent of her hair and share the magic of the scene.

Nothing but romantic illusion, he reminded himself, fingering the silver key in his pocket. He should be dealing with the reality of snarled rush-hour traffic. He stood and lifted his overcoat from the coat tree. "Get your coat and I'll walk you to the parking lot."

"You don't have to—"

"I know. I'm leaving, too. We're probably parked in the same row."

She hesitated, then sighed. "All right, I'll meet you at the door."

Blake passed slowly through the suite to the front, pondering his restlessness. That he'd wanted to kiss Wren was totally unacceptable. He'd probably just imagined that she'd wanted to kiss him, too. Irritated, he flipped off the light switch.

She had obliged him with an alarmingly detailed description of her domestic dream. Another firm snap punctuated the silence.

Suddenly there in the semi-darkness, the full impact of their conversation hit. *She wanted marriage... and children.* And he didn't.

That was the bottom line. He flicked the last light off.

Sparkling snow danced around the globes lighting the walk to the parking lot, brightening the night sky like a row of haloed moons. Wren walked ahead of Blake, willing her awareness away from him, focusing instead on the fat clusters of white flakes drifting down to brush her face and cling to her eyelashes.

Someone had shoveled the walk earlier, but a thin layer of new snow muffled their footsteps. No sound interrupted the wintry hush. The night seemed to hold its breath.

Glancing back, she could see the stern planes of Blake's face absorbing the pale light like pewter. The sight made her heart ache.

Blake hadn't spoken since she'd met him at the front door, and she understood why. She'd known perfectly well that he wasn't ready to hear about a home—especially not about babies. As if that weren't bad enough, she'd had to lecture him about the influence of parents.

If only she'd learn to stop talking sooner! Every time she made a little ground with him, she managed to say something to throw it all away.

She simply had to stop prodding him, give him time to accept her work, to admit that she was good. To agree that she'd make a good business partner.

"Where's your car, Wren?"

Blake's voice rumbled like distant thunder, sending echoes zigzagging through her, reminding her of when he'd murmured her name in his office...when she'd all but paced right into his arms. The memory still made her tremble.

"Over there, by the light." She pointed to the little red car covered with a layer of white.

"Ah, yes. The graduation car. I'd forgotten. I'll help you clean it off."

Blake was obviously trying to get them back on comfortable ground. She opened the trunk and pulled out snow-cleaning equipment.

"You brush, I'll scrape," Blake said, taking the scraper and moving to the front windows.

Wren started on the back.

"Now that you've got this little beauty, have you decided what else you'll spend your trust money on?" Blake called to her.

Making friendly, *safe* conversation, she thought. "No, I'm still getting used to the idea of having money. I was so shocked when the Colonel said he'd invested Dad's insurance benefits and paid my tuition himself. I never dreamed—"

"Falls under the heading of Commanding Officer Repays Recruit For Saving His Life In Nam. The Colonel didn't know how to thank your dad. He doesn't do feelings—except with money."

Wren stopped brushing and watched Blake work his way down the other side of the car, unaware of her scrutiny. He'd never revealed such rancor toward the

Colonel before. It helped explain the rocky defenses he'd built, but not how she could break through them.

"Almost done. That should get you home safely."

Snow speckled his hair, and Wren thought of reaching to sweep away the white, to soothe away his hurt, leaving only damp butterscotch waves and that rogue swatch of hair falling into hopefully less-bitter eyes. Instead, she buried the impulse in her pocket, searching for her keys.

Blake thumped the brush and scraper against a tire, then dropped both pieces into the trunk and slammed the lid with a thunk.

"Oh..." The keys she was struggling to fish from her pocket slipped from her gloved fingers and disappeared into the snow.

"I'll get them."

Before she knew it, Blake knelt beside her.

"Got 'em." Rising, he twirled the ring around his wet index finger and reached out to help her up.

She knew right away she shouldn't have taken his hand. When she straightened, he didn't let go. If anything, his grip tightened, the warmth of his hand seeping through her glove. In a faraway part of her mind, it occurred to her that they both must have stopped breathing, because no puffs of vapor filled the narrow space between them. She could see his dusk-blue eyes clearly, could read turmoil there.

And though she knew she shouldn't, she lifted her face, felt the cold night air as she moistened her lips.

She heard her heart repeating, *Kiss me... Please.*

Chapter Five

"You have snowflakes on your eyelashes," Blake murmured, reaching toward her as if to touch a snowy butterfly. He gazed down at her, his face burnished by the glow of the parking lot light.

She saw him waver, saw conflict darken his eyes to the color of fall smoke. "Blake?" she breathed, as if saying his name might cast a spell to hold him there.

He drew the backs of his fingers slowly down her cheek, tracing a tingling path, awakening something buoyant and shimmering inside her. Which of them worked this sorcery? she wondered.

His finger curled under her chin, warm and coaxing, calling up spirits that danced within her and reflected in his shadowed eyes. As had happened once before, she imagined something soft and tender brush her lips. A phantom kiss.

Her heart all but stopped, waiting, willing him to dip his head. She saw him consider, refuse, then yield without choosing, his mouth brushing her half-parted lips, so warm, so devastatingly gentle, that all her own resolves failed.

His mouth moved against hers, nipping, tasting, destroying whatever evanescent thought she might have had to make him stop. He was shaman and sorcerer, but this kiss was no fantasy. It was sweet and soft, more tender than she'd ever imagined in all the nights she'd longed for him ... a girl whose body had trembled on the brink of what it would mean to be a woman, to be loved as a woman.

But those were the inexperienced conjurings of a child. Blake's kiss was profoundly gentle, but when his hands moved to her shoulders, he grasped her fiercely with a hold both feral and restrained, with heat she could feel as if he'd touched bare skin.

Did he stay her to keep her from fleeing, or to hold himself back? She couldn't be sure, but the promise of his passion made her tremble.

Almost as if against his will, he drew her to him, no longer asking, but giving and taking the full measure of their kiss. She yielded because she had no choice. Because she'd wanted this. She'd waited for this.

Her lips sought the shape of his hollows, and she tasted him, sought his flavor with the shy tip of her tongue. He inhaled sharply, snatching breath from her mouth before his arms embraced her, pressing her against him until she was lost, floating in a spell of enchantment, in the heat of his body, in the taste of almonds and the fleeting scent of spice and masculinity. Lost in a fire that coiled through her like molten starlight in spite of the wintery cold.

She wanted to hold him, to touch him, to feel the solid proof of him. Raising her hands, she hesitated, then slid them up the front of his coat.

At the brush of her glove on the back of his neck, he stilled, then broke from the kiss. As if chastened, he rested his forehead against hers, leaving her lips both burning and cold, moisture gathering in her eyes. She could feel his fingers working her shoulders, fighting a silent battle.

Before she could tilt her chin to capture him again, he stepped away. His hands disappeared into his coat pockets.

A familiar retreat, she thought hazily, shivering from the cold chasm that loomed between them. A strategy she'd tried herself. A withdrawal she should have made.

She should have said a fast goodbye, climbed into her car, made a swift retreat. That way she wouldn't have ended up battling both fire and ice, in danger of shattering into shards of broken dreams.

"I apologize, Wren. This never should have happened." Blake's voice was ragged, his eyes gray with anger as he moved another step away. Growling to clear his throat, he looked down to the silvery key he'd pulled from his pocket. "I assure you, it won't happen again."

Numb, she watched him rasp the key with his thumb while she struggled, gathering her trembling under control. Surely the key was a talisman with powers to protect him. Or maybe... maybe he was guarding the key to his heart.

Turning away, Blake unlocked the door to her car. "Get in, Wren. Start the engine."

God help her, his withdrawal was complete. He was outdoing even the Colonel, his command so gruff, its harshness stung. *Blake, please don't do this.* She searched his face for some hint of the passion she'd felt, but he refused to look at her. He'd turned to cold lava—dark and rough and forbidding.

"Blake?"

"I want to see your car running and you driving away."

The man was just plain hardheaded, as stubborn as a Missouri mule! "Yes, *sir!*" She spun in the snow and threw herself into the car.

Backing up, she watched Blake trudge to his four-by-four and climb in. When she heard the engine roar, she stomped her own accelerator and swerved out of the parking lot, one thought repeating in her head.

What was she going to do if she couldn't move this immovable mountain after all?

"Come on, Wren. I know right where the class is."

In her purple parka, Ruby looked fit for the Klondike, but she swept through the glass doors of her favorite fitness center as if she wore gossamer and silk.

Smiling with affection, Wren followed her into a reception area of navy carpet and teal chairs. Exercise equipment filled the rooms on each side.

"The prenatal class is downstairs," Ruby said. "I see them every week when I work out."

Exactly where the instructor had told Wren to meet her. She followed Ruby down the white-tiled stairs into an enormous open space that looked like a metal jungle. Overhead parallel strips of lights and chrome glistened in the ceiling, and exercise equipment, like robotic skeletons, covered the floor in a frozen dance.

Everything looked upscale and sleek. Like the bodies that worked out there.

Like the corded arms and flexing back muscles of the man on the piece of equipment across the way. Wren's heartbeat faltered. What was Blake doing here?

"By the way," Ruby said, "I forgot to tell you, Blake called for directions. He said he wanted to help."

Then she wasn't hallucinating after all, hadn't just conjured him up out of two days of earth-moving thinking. After dodging her since Monday night, as if she had a case of the chicken pox, now he wanted to help? He must have decided her suggestion to improve the sacred bottom line warranted lifting the quarantine he'd imposed, at least temporarily. "Good. We'll put him to work." She watched his face tighten with concentration and his jaw clench as he pressed bars of angled metal together in front of his chest. As if he needed to improve his strength. From what she'd experienced, he was already plenty strong enough to ward off the most aggressive of Amazons much less one fairly small but very determined mountain-town woman.

She watched with fascination as his body tensed against the resistance of the machine. This wasn't the setting she'd anticipated when she'd begun to formulate a new plan, but it didn't matter. He could pump iron all he wanted, because she'd been thinking about flexing a few muscles herself. An idea had begun to take shape in the past two days, a plan that would surpass even the tactics of Hannibal. And Hannibal was a man who knew how to deal with mountains.

Blake stood up from the pec-dec and moved to the lat pulldown, concentrating on resetting the weights. What he really needed was about twenty laps around the track followed by an icy shower. Because when Wren had appeared, skimming down the stairs like a gymnast, her yellow-and-black sweat suit failing to conceal her alluring curves, he'd known right away that the distance he'd kept between them these past two days had accomplished exactly nothing. *Nada.* Zip. He was just as intrigued, just as bewitched, as he'd been since... since he'd discovered she was no longer a kid.

He couldn't keep her out of his mind. If he tried to concentrate on work, he would drift into upbraiding himself for kissing her. If he reminded himself his only business with her *was* business, suddenly her dreams of home and children rose to plague him.

Every time he thought about her, he saw dark teasing eyes and lush full lips, felt her kiss.

Drawing in a sharp breath, he shifted to bicep curls and a tougher direction for his thoughts. Staying away from her had been a mistake; he'd realized that this afternoon. He was making too much of a few simple kisses. What he needed was to be around her *more,* to be reminded of her constant laughter, to chafe at her impractical optimism. Let familiarity breed, if not contempt, then at least disinterest.

"Reporting for duty, Bird Woman."

Blake's head shot up at the offensive nickname ringing across the room. What was Jaime doing here? Wasn't he supposed to be on the telephones in the evenings? Combing fingers back through his hair, Blake abandoned the equipment and strode across the floor toward them.

"Blake, there you are." Aunt Ruby waved. "You'd better be my partner because Wren's already been claimed." A decided sparkle brightened her silvery blue eyes.

Blake frowned. It wasn't like him to be impatient with his aunt, but this was hardly the place for matchmaking.

"We won't work in teams," Wren countered, sounding more confident even than he'd remembered, and very much in charge. "It's not efficient." She slanted him a radiant smile that made no attempt to disguise the tilt of her chin. "We'll interview on those benches by the wall. If you're here to help, Blake, would you run through the questionnaire with Ruby? She offered to help out, too. Jaime, please check upstairs for Lisa. She's my other interviewer tonight. I'll let the instructor know we're ready."

Blake's reaction was immediate and troublesome. All the stewing he'd done about how she might act toward him since the other evening had been a waste of time. She was all business, and he should be feeling relieved, not somehow dispossessed.

He started through the questionnaire with Ruby, but his attention kept stealing back to Wren. She seemed so assured speaking to the pregnant women marching on treadmill machines at the back of the room. As if nothing had happened between them. Which was the way it should be, because what had happened between them was nothing more than—

"Blake!"

"What?"

"For the third time—" Ruby raised three fingers and shook them at him "—I can read the questionnaire perfectly well by myself." She studied him, the lines at the corners of her eyes crinkled with curiosity. "Are *you* ready? Because here comes Wren."

She descended on them like a locomotive with five cabooses. "Okay, Jaime, I want you on that end. Lisa next, then Ruby. Blake and I will work this end. Ladies, please pick an interviewer. We won't keep you long."

Trying to keep his attention from Wren became abruptly less difficult when he saw a woman in a pink T-shirt, her stomach grown round like a medicine ball, leave the group of expectant mothers to steer straight toward him. She smiled boldly and tossed her short red hair, and he stifled an impulse to flee. Why did he attract the women most likely to go into immediate labor? Did he look like a damn baby doctor?

And why did pregnant women always seem to rest their hands on their stomachs as if they guarded a secret? The observation increased his uneasiness.

Dredging up a welcome, he directed the woman to sit. The minute he straddled the bench to face her, he knew he'd made a mistake. He had difficulty enough keeping his eyes from her roundness, without having Wren seated behind her where he could watch every tilt of her head, every encouraging smile.

He couldn't remember one interview in the past that had been this tough. How was he supposed to take decent notes when there were so many distractions, when his lady absently caressed her round stomach while she answered questions? It was too intimate a gesture, yet he couldn't help but recognize the gentle care, the unconscious nurturing. In spite of his discomfort, her automatic soothing touched him.

Wren and her interviewee burst into laughter, and he glanced up to determine what had caused her bright cascade. He was shocked to find he was waiting to hear it again. That wasn't the effect she was supposed to have on him.

Wren's lady rose at the same time his did, leaving a space between them that felt like a canyon.

"I didn't think you'd be here tonight," she said so quietly she might have been musing to herself. Yet there was a question in her mellow voice that unnerved him further.

"Just consider this my contribution to the success of your probationary project."

Only Wren could look both vexed and fearless at the same time. She smiled, and he sensed again his world slipping out of control.

"Thanks, Blake. Consider the Nestlings account my contribution to the growth of *our* company."

There was that tilt to her chin again . . . almost as if she were issuing a challenge.

"Excuse me, should I sit here?"

He dragged his attention from Wren to acknowledge the woman in front of him. "Yes, please sit down."

Wren had never been one for subtlety. When she wasn't teasing, she was usually blunt to a fault, so why did he get the ominous feeling that she wasn't teasing, that she was dead serious about her meager ownership in his company?

"They said you wanted to ask some questions."

Blake forced his attention to his new interviewee. She sat braced on one arm, her head cocked inquisitively to one side, her ponytail falling over one shoulder. Her oversize blue T-shirt and shiny tights made her look terribly young.

Like Wren. The Wren he used to know. Except that this young woman, just as all the others who sought him out like bears to a hive of honey, would be a mother *very* soon. He squelched a groan and started down the list of questions.

"My first baby," the young woman answered. "We already know it's a girl. We're going to name her Emma. Tom, that's my husband, he's so excited."

And this young thing was so proud, Blake realized. They all seemed to be, and so serenely protective of their ripe bodies, so full of anticipation.

"And what would you like to see available that you haven't found in the stores?" he asked.

"Gosh, I don't know...."

"*I* do," the woman sitting with Wren chimed in. "A tummy sling."

"A *tummy sling?*" Wren repeated. "Don't you dare write that down, Blake. This one's mine. Please, go on!" She waved her pencil to prompt her.

"I like to play tennis, but at this stage—" Wren's woman patted her tummy "—I'm too...voluminous? I need something like extralarge jockey shorts with very wide suspenders to keep this guppy from bouncing when *I* do." She patted her stomach.

He was getting a little more used to all this body talk, enough so that he could join their laughter.

"That's great," Wren encouraged. "Anything else? Blake gets the rest of your ideas."

Wren smiled across at him, and he realized he'd give her all the ideas if she would smile like that again. This definitely wasn't the effect she was supposed to be having on him.

"Oh!" Blake's young woman inhaled abruptly. She leaned back and pressed her hand to her stomach.

His attention flew from her hand to Wren, but she didn't seem concerned.

He knew it. The woman was going to have her baby right *here*. Right *now*. "I'll go call a doctor."

Still holding her stomach, the woman managed a laugh. "No, no, she's just kicking. Tom says she'll be a soccer player." She smoothed the folds from her T-shirt and pointed.

My God, he could see movement! A slight thumping beneath the taut surface of the fabric, as if a tiny being were trying to get out.

"Look!" Wren's amazement rang in her voice. "Could I . . . ?"

"Sure." The woman took Wren's slender hand and laid it on her stomach.

"I can *feel* her," Wren murmured. She turned delighted eyes to Blake, eyes glowing with wonder.

He heard her marvel at this new life, saw the joy shimmering in her eyes. But he wasn't prepared to see her longing, nor to watch her cup her hand with the other as if to capture the flicker of life she'd felt like a tiny firefly. He didn't understand the ache it stirred in him.

"Blake, do you want—?"

"Here."

Before he could protest, the young woman took his hand and placed it where Wren's had lain. Against the soft blue of her rounded T-shirt, his hand looked big-boned and blocky, like a hammer on a piece of velvet. Beneath his fingers he felt a strong kick, a life force declaring itself.

The sensation tapped at his fingertips, quieting everything within him to the stillness of a cathedral.

This, he suddenly understood, was the meaning of reverence. A swell of emotion knotted in his throat.

What if this were his child? His wife? Was this a portion of what he would feel? The thought came to him unbidden, made him turn to look again at Wren. She was watching him with the same awe-filled wonder.

"Thank you."

Wren directed the words simply to the young lady, but her soft doe eyes stirred the same desire in him he'd felt for her standing in the wintry wonderland of the parking lot. The feelings he'd come here to lose.

"I keep hoping she'll wear herself out so she'll sleep nights after she arrives." The woman patted her stomach.

Blake was too stunned to join their laughter. Far from breeding disinterest, this kind of familiarity with Wren was something he didn't know how to handle.

"Do either of you have any other ideas?" Wren asked, directing them back to the questionnaire.

Even in his distracted state, the smoothness of her transition impressed him. In spite of her emotions, she hadn't let herself stray far from business.

"Yes," Blake's lady answered. "My husband wants a class on how to deliver babies."

Her husband. In the back of his mind something stirred, like a word he was searching for and couldn't recall. "Tell me more," he said, and felt Wren watching him.

"If the baby decides to show up early, Tom says he'd like to do more than just fetch hot water and clean sheets. After all, he's the one who got us into this condition in the first place."

The woman laughed again, but this time their humor didn't include him. It was a women's joke that left out men in general, almost as if this miracle of making a baby were an exclusive thing, too complex for mere males to share—except for the kickoff and the cheering at the goal line.

Suddenly he felt the clean sharp bite of anger. He grasped at the security of a familiar emotion, relieved to have the clarity of principled indignation to cling to in the maelstrom of feelings the evening had churned.

There was a serious problem here. In the whole time they'd been working on the Nestlings account, they'd interviewed not one man. Wren hadn't even thought about the fathers. She'd overlooked half the baby-making population.

How could he have overlooked it? The answer was too damn obvious. Ever since they'd started on the Nestlings account, he'd been getting sentimental over an event that had been happening since the beginning of time. He'd gotten downright sloppy over something that occurred all over the world.

Having babies just wasn't that big a deal. He needed to stop letting these women—this woman—unbalance him. He needed to regain his footing.

Even as he rode the swell of his anger, he knew he was overreacting, knew he was grasping at a raft of weak arguments held together by shaky justifications. A raft that was likely to sink beneath him. But he couldn't stop himself. He didn't know how else to defend his heart against her.

As the business owner, he had to take the blame. But if Wren was going to learn, and most especially, if she was going to play shareholder with him, he'd make damn sure she was the one to set things right.

Chapter Six

"Wren, honey, I have to leave."

Wren looked up from the fitness center bench to find Ruby zipping her purple parka, her furry white hood already framing the silver of her hair.

"Hold on a minute till I pull these questionnaires together and I'll be ready."

"I forgot to tell you, hon. My bingo starts in half an hour, and I have to pick up Helen."

"But, Ruby—"

"It was fun, Wren." Ruby waved as she side-stepped across the floor. "You can catch a ride from Blake." She turned and started up the stairs.

A ride! No wonder Ruby had offered to help. She had, without a doubt, gotten the idea to volunteer about two seconds after Blake called for directions. Ruby had driven her here intending to abandon her.

"*Ru-by,*" Wren said with a sigh, watching the slight woman disappear up the stairs. She loved her dearly, but there were times when she could have happily wrung her neck.

"I'll drive you home, Wren."

She turned to see if by some quantum leap the Colonel had beamed in right beside her. Blake sounded like his father again, and about as grumpy as Ebenezer Scrooge.

"Thanks, Blake, but I can get a ride with Lisa...or Jaime."

Blake's nostrils actually flared. Just minutes ago he'd been all but entranced by the sight of a kicking tadpole. Why, suddenly, would he be angry?

"I'll take you. I have something to discuss with you."

As if the hard edge in his voice weren't enough, she could tell by the taut lines of his mouth that the matter wasn't open for debate. Whatever was on Blake's mind, the weather had certainly changed—from a promise of spring back to the cold days of winter.

Slipping into her jacket, she chanced a sideways glance and saw that his eyes had darkened to the color of a mountain lake before snow. His attitude was just as chilling. He looked as if this might be one of those rare times when his storm reached blizzard proportions.

Without a word, he held open the exit door. All the way to the parking lot he didn't speak, just moved her along purposefully, his hand firm on her elbow.

She would have much preferred him to bluster. At least then he'd let go of some of those emotions, misdirected though they might be. She hated it when he didn't talk.

"Blake, I've been walking by myself for quite a few years now."

He didn't answer, only marched her along with the look of a peeved big brother. Or a fire-and-brimstone preacher, she thought, resisting the impulse to tell him so, to try again to make him smile.

When they reached his four-by-four, he released her to unlock the door, but he didn't let go of his restraint. Even after he raced the engine and sped out into traffic, she could see the muscles of his jaw working.

Lull before the storm, she thought impatiently. Whatever it was that was causing his barometer to crash, if he was going to thunder, she wished he'd get on with it. The few times he'd ever been truly angry with her hadn't lasted long... and he'd at least unleashed some passion.

"Don't you think it's about time you let me know what this is all about?"

For a long moment he didn't answer. In the dim panel lights she could see him grip the steering wheel. Not half as effective a release as the pacing he'd be doing if they were in his office. As if to figure out how near his lightning would strike, she found herself counting, *One one-thousand, two one-thousand...*

When he spoke, it was with a rumble. "I don't like what I learn each time I work these questionnaires."

She could tell he was headed toward full lecture mode. Good thing they were in the privacy of the Rover, because his voice resounded from the closed windows, and a shock of amber hair fell across his forehead. He was working up steam now.

"Those women will all be mothers...."

"Some of them already are."

"But they all work."

She bit her tongue to keep from tossing back, "Being a mother *is* work." Whatever this conversation was about, she didn't think it was that. She'd never known Blake to stereotype women.

"And they plan to *continue* working, even after their babies are born."

"That seems to be the pattern nowadays," she ventured, waiting for a better sense of why he was building such a charge.

"A mother should be with her children, not off somewhere pursuing her own thing while the kid's dumped on someone else." As if to punctuate the point, he wrenched the steering wheel in a turn. The Rover slipped a little as they passed between the brick columns that marked Ruby's entrance.

So Blake's encounter with Ryan was still stirring too many memories. Was that what this was about? "Nowadays, both parents are pretty involved with their kids, Blake. Dads pitch in a lot. It's a real partnership." She hadn't intended the word and watched his eyes for a reaction.

They remained remote and edged with darkness, but he didn't withdraw further into his usual fortification. Racing up the curved drive, he braked in front of the wide front porch. With the engine still running, he turned a stony face to her.

"So you think fathers are an important part of the formula?"

"Blake, that goes without—"

"—without saying? You didn't bother to say anything about a father when you were telling me you wanted a whole lot of kids. You never mentioned a partner."

"You didn't ask about—"

"Well, I'm asking now. How important do you think the man is in this so-called partnership?"

"I think he's *very* important. It's pretty difficult to make a kid without one." Her attempt at humor failed miserably. His indignation was too well entrenched.

"Why didn't you include the fathers in your research?"

In her imagination, Wren heard a glass-rattling thunderclap. Blake's lightning had finally struck.

"Blake, if you read my proposal you'll see—"

"I've read it, Wren. No men were interviewed in the first three projects, which means if Lisle Mason decides not to continue, he has *no* feedback from the fathers. You've overlooked *half* the buyer population. That's ineffectual marketing research, Wren. Brockman Incorporated doesn't do ineffectual research." Blake's glare didn't relent, any more than his self-righteous outrage. His eyes shone dark as sapphires in the shadows of the car.

It was the same look that always triggered her frustration, mingled with anticipation. Blake harbored such simmering intensity... and spent it on too many of the wrong commitments.

"I *assumed* Mr. Mason would accept the whole proposal," she said calmly, meeting his scowl with a steady gaze. She held her breath, waiting for his response.

"You should know better than to assume *anything* in the business world."

More was coming; she could tell by the way he shifted to confront her.

"If you get so wrapped up in expectant mothers and babies that you make an oversight like this, I have to question how suited you are for this job."

"Blake, how can you say that when this account has brought in—"

"I have to question your commitment to my business."

So there it was. It was his business he fought for. Expect that his anger was too great, his accusations too overblown. He was protesting far too much, firing cannonballs at sparrows. A sure sign that she was making inroads through his defenses. The possibility spurred her courage.

Blake unsnapped his seat belt and opened his door.

"Wait a minute. Is that all? Aren't we going to discuss this?"

"There's nothing to discuss." He slid away from her and set one foot out on the drive.

"Oh, no, you don't, Blake Brockman." She grabbed his arm and tugged. "Don't you dump me off at the door like a foundling without even giving me a chance to answer." She gave his arm another pull, and then he wasn't outside in the cold anymore, but there, beside her, wedged shoulder-to-shoulder against her.

He turned as if in slow motion, his face set in a ferocious glare just inches from hers.

Dear God, only a fool would grab a growling lion. Instinctively, she put a hand on his chest to pacify him. She could feel his body tense, see his jaw knot and unknot. But his eyes belied everything.

In their turbulent blue depths, his anger relented, gave way to grudging admiration and a hint of humor, that droll amusement that denied absolutely any similarity to the Colonel and captured her heart all over again. She couldn't help thinking that what she'd been hearing were the rumbling protests of a slowly moving mountain.

But his eyes didn't move. She couldn't have escaped their fateful magnetism even if she'd wanted to. She saw him change again, take on a different kind of fierceness—the look she'd seen that night in the parking lot, when, for a brief shining moment, she'd dreamed he'd wanted her.

"Blake..." She'd meant to be firm, but his name came out as a whisper.

He exhaled sharply, his heat skimming her cheek, feathering the hair beside her ear, sending sparks of pleasure skating across her shoulders.

She was afraid to move, to disturb the tension that crackled between them, afraid to breathe, to inhale the potent scent of musk and almonds. He held her gaze until he'd closed the charged gap between them to brush her lips with his mouth.

"Blake...?"

"Don't talk." He shifted, and she felt his fingers trace flame across her temple to weave fire into her hair. He pulled her nearer, tasting the curves and creases of her mouth, hungrily drawing her lips between his as if sipping the sweetness of tropical fruit.

She felt limp and deliciously drunk, full of the need to kiss him back, robbed of the strength to stop herself.

"Blake," she whispered between hard kisses, "the rest of the projects will—"

"No promises." His tongue sought the soft smooth flesh just inside her lips. He caressed her there as if discovering for the first time the silky texture of ice cream.

"Blake...?" She struggled to keep from reaching for him, from sending him running as her touch had done before.

"Just do it." His hands moved to her shoulders and began etching slow fire down her arms. Even through the thickness of her jacket, she felt his heat as he paused near her breasts, felt her nipples tighten in anticipation.

She gasped in spite of herself. "The next project...is a Prepared...Childbirth...class. The fathers will be there."

His hands tensed on her arms, and she knew something was wrong. She fought the need to arch against him, to slide her arms around his neck, to pull him against her and kiss him senseless. To make him let go of his childhood yearnings and his grown-up defenses—his pointless self-imposed fortresses—if only for a little while. To make him forget everything except what they could discover together. But she could tell it was already too late.

Blake sat back and swiped a hand through the shock of hair on his forehead.

Hair the color of wild honey, she mused languorously. This man needed to make wild honey.

"Blake?"

But he was gone, vaulting out of the car and around to tug her door open. Without a word, he walked her up the broad stairs and across the porch of the snow-covered two-story house.

This time she held her key firmly in hand, ready to unlock the door before he could offer.

"As for the company," she said, as if nothing had interrupted their discussion, "I'm *very* serious about my commitment there."

If you're going to gamble, be bold, her dad had taught her, a lesson she'd used often in poker *and* in life.

Tilting her chin, she let her tongue play along her swollen lips. When she saw his eyes stray reluctantly to her mouth, she smiled. "The fact is, Blake, I'm thinking about buying some of your company's outstanding shares."

He never should have gone to the fitness center on Wednesday. He damn sure shouldn't be here tonight. Why were there so many people at the hospital on a Friday night?

Blake stomped the Rover's brakes and backed up. Damned if he hadn't almost passed a parking place . . . all because he'd let the Colonel talk him into sharing the guardianship of a little brown bird years ago. Just one more thing he never should have done. He didn't need Wren complicating his life any more than she already had.

Climbing out of the four-by-four, he trudged through the snowy parking lot, dread and anticipation dogging his feet. Spending another evening with Wren and her pregnant mothers was the last thing he should be doing, given that when he did, he ended up kissing her, ended up wanting her. She was wheedling her way into his existence, and he didn't know how to stop her, wasn't sure anymore if he wanted to.

He shoved through the hospital doors and followed the signs down the hall. Hopefully the class would be over so he could get involved in the interviews without spending time with her, because spending time with her was becoming too hazardous. She wanted too many things he couldn't give her. He had no place for her in his future.

For that matter, he wasn't at all sure of the wisdom of a place for her at his office. Lately she'd been sounding as if she meant to become some kind of partner. He shoved his hands deeper into his pockets, sought the rough edge of his silver key. Another problem he'd have to deal with. Soon.

"Blake, you made it. I was getting worried." Wren waved from the bench where she sat with an expectant young couple. Her smile reached her eyes as a question.

A careful smile—he didn't want that, either. He didn't want her walking on eggshells while he decided what to do about her, what to do about himself.

With effort he shifted his attention to the pregnant woman next to Wren, then had to stop himself from staring. She was cradling a teddy bear! Stuffed animals seemed to be the order of the evening. A large purple dinosaur peeked out of another woman's tote bag, and pink rabbit ears flopped under a man's arm. The hall was lined with critter-toting couples...and Jaime Sandoval, not far from Wren, interviewing a man and woman with a large stuffed dalmatian.

"We can use your help." Wren rose and brought Blake a clipboard. "Jaime and I are the only interviewers."

He nodded and beat a hasty retreat before her appraising smile weakened his resolve to avoid her, especially since Jaime hovered so near. Armed with the clipboard, Blake joined a young-looking couple and tried to immerse himself in an interview, but the questions weren't enough to hold his focus, to keep him from watching Wren.

He'd seen her in sweatshirts and jeans for years, but even in casual clothes she looked different these days—bright red warm-up suit, dark hair rippling with untamed waves, glowing face. A lot like the pregnant women, but prettier.

She and Jaime could easily be one of the young couples-in-waiting this evening. All they needed was their own stuffed animal. Instead of amusing him, the image recharged his lingering agitation. Nowadays he seemed to overreact to everything. And nothing.

At least he had one genuine issue he could act on tonight. He directed his next question to the young father in front of him. "What would *you* like to see made available to help new *fathers?*" he asked the young man.

"I don't know. Maybe a substitute coach?" he ducked an imaginary swat from the girl beside him and smiled sheepishly.

"Coach?"

"Birth coach. That's what we're called in these classes. I'm…a little nervous about being there when the baby is…coming."

"He's a *lot* nervous." The girl laughed. "But he's doing great in the class. He's a great partner. You'll be just fine, honey." Standing on tiptoe, she pecked him on the cheek.

"Okay, folks, class time." A tall woman in white slacks and lab coat strode toward them down the hall. The resident stork, Blake thought, though he could tell from the conviction in her walk that he wouldn't want to be caught saying so aloud.

He watched the young man put his arm around his very pregnant partner and walk her away. The kid might be scared to participate in his baby's birth, but the look on his face when he smiled at his wife explained his presence here.

It was easy enough to sympathize with the guy's discomfort. Blake sure as hell wouldn't want to be in a breathing class, either.

"How'd the questions go, Ms. March?" The tall woman opened the door to a room across the hall.

"We interviewed about half the couples. Fran, this is Jaime Sandoval...and Blake Brockman. Fran's the instructor."

Fran nodded to Jaime, then paused to study Blake, a probing examination that made him wonder if she'd read his mind about being the in-house delivery bird.

"Why don't you stay through the class? Everyone gave permission last week. They might come up with some ideas for you while they're practicing. You can finish the interviews afterward."

"That's a wonderful idea," Wren said, then turned to Jaime.

"Can't, Bird Woman. Finals tomorrow. But I'll be back after class to finish the interviews."

Blake rankled at the disappointment on her face. When she turned to him, he was more displeased to see doubt.

"Blake?"

"I'll stay."

Damn. He'd had no intentions of sticking around to watch a lot of women clutching stuffed animals and blowing at imaginary candles. But he saw elation brighten Wren's eyes and knew he'd relented just for that. Knew, for the first time, that he was in much deeper trouble then he'd realized. He'd lost control of his decisions. He should leave . . . while he still could.

He watched Fran disappear into the room followed by everyone else. For a moment, he stood alone in the empty hall considering the path to guaranteed complications, then the elevators to retreat. Jamming the clipboard under his arm, he stalked through the doorway.

The room was large, with desks pushed against the walls and beanbag chairs dotting the floor like giant colored marshmallows.

"Why don't you two take that bag?" Fran pointed to a green mound in the far corner. "You can practice along with us . . . for future events." She winked at Blake.

"There are no beanbags in my future." That was one decision he wouldn't change, no matter how he reacted to Wren's kisses or her tentative smiles.

He turned away from Fran's measured inspection to watch the men help their women down into the colorful beanbags and sit beside them on the carpeted floor. He glanced at the big video screen, the windowless beige walls, the pictures of babies and pregnant women hung at intervals about the room. Then he made the mistake of looking across at Wren.

Curled up in the beanbag, she looked petite and dainty among the other women, her eyes already eager with curiosity. A little red fish in the middle of a school of whales.

And the fathers? Captives . . . longing for the freedom of the open sea.

Damn, he was letting his cynicism get out of hand, behaving downright churlish and suffering an attack of guilt, which he probably deserved. In a setting as antiseptic as this, he shouldn't have to worry about unruly libidinous surges. What harm could come from just sitting with her?

"Let's get started on your relaxation," Fran directed while she fiddled with a tape recorder. Fuzzy static faded, and the sounds of new age music filled the room.

"Partners, on the floor. Practice your breathing and your imaging . . ." She drew the words out like a hypnotist.

"Come on, Blake. Sit down," Wren whispered. "Like that." She pointed to the couple next to them.

He'd have to have been blind to miss the eagerness in her eyes. "What are they, friends of the zoo?" he muttered. The man and woman sat facing each other, legs crossed, with a fat white teddy bear between them.

"No, they're friends of each other. They're partners," she shot back. "The bear's for focus." Sliding from the beanbag, she sat on the floor and crossed her legs.

Against his better judgment, he mirrored her movements, wishing he had a bear for focus, too, instead of Wren, sitting smack in front of him, earnestly waiting to become involved in the activities. "Clan of the Teddy Bears," he growled, half amused at the idea. "Now what?"

"Do what they do."

The suggestion sounded simple enough until he turned to watch the couple. The woman was breathing slowly and evenly, and the man paced himself with her, breath for breath. Their eyes held one another, and their mouths softened into something that was more than a smile. It was almost as if they shared a secret, as if they somehow communicated without words.

He couldn't do that, not with Wren. Not for an hour. Not for five *minutes*. Because he was pretty sure his reaction would be graphic. And embarrassing. He hadn't come here for this.

"Wren, I came to work, not to play Spin-The-Teddy-Bear. I'll come back when the class lets out."

"Blake, wait." She reached to grab his arm, but stopped herself in midmotion. Touching Blake always seemed to be the wrong thing to do, as if bridging the space between them were tantamount to breaching the walls of his fortress. He had to leave his castle by his own choice. She just wished he wouldn't take quite so long.

"Okay." Fran's firm voice overrode the soothing violins of the music. "Moms, lie down, heads and knees elevated with your pillows. Dads, on your knees beside her. Ms. March, you and your partner can follow along. Use these pillows."

Wren caught two pillows as they flew through the air. Mentally, she willed Blake to stay. He'd been such a good sport so far with the Nestlings activities, he just couldn't walk out now.

Blake frowned, but she could tell it was more from habit than resolve. "It wouldn't be polite to leave now," she whispered, settling onto the pillows.

The lines between his brows deepened, and she held her breath. At last he eased down to his knees.

"I don't think Fran's into polite." A shade of reluctant humor crept into his voice. "Just remember, you owe me a couple of really miserable field assignments."

In spite of his scowl, he was teasing her! "Send me into the sweaty depths of the stadium locker rooms if you want," she whispered back, immensely relieved.

"If you want beef, I'll send you to a meat-packing plant."

"Simon Legree."

"No talking during relaxation." Fran looked their way. "Moms, remember your cleansing breaths. Dads, you're going to keep her focused. Use your animals or hold her hand. Or rub her tummy." Fran turned a knob on the wall and the lights dimmed.

"Still here?" Wren whispered, peering up at Blake, fighting a grin.

"After meat packers, you go directly to sewer cleaners," he rasped back. "On-site."

This time, she laughed out loud. "Sorry." She cringed and waved to Fran.

"Okay, dads, hold up fingers to let Mom know how many deep breaths you want to see. Moms, nice and relaxed. Think about the breezes in that high mountain meadow...."

Wren tried to mimic the slow easy rhythm of the woman next to them. It was hard to relax with Blake so near, but she eased back onto the pillows and risked looking up at him, still half expecting to see him fleeing through the door.

Instead, he raised his hand and held up four fingers.

The gesture spun happiness all the way to her toes. This was more than she'd dared dream of. Blake was playing along, letting himself get involved. Her reluctant knight was risking a step outside the fortress walls.

Without thinking, she reached out and clasped his other hand.

Chapter Seven

Blake didn't start. He didn't pull away. Somewhere in a distant part of his mind, where he still clung to reality, he even acknowledged a degree of pride. Somehow he was managing not to take to his heels and run as Wren wove her slender fingers through his. Somehow he was disguising the pulse roaring through his veins while she clung to him as if her own baby struggled to make its entrance into the world.

Play along, he counseled himself. *Stay calm.* Wren had an overactive imagination. She always threw herself into these things wholeheartedly—he knew that. She was having the time of her life, and he was just a stage prop. That's why he was here.

If Jaime had stayed, she'd be going through the same histrionics with him. She'd be holding *his* gaze, clutching *his* hand.

Fat lot of help that thought was. Damn it, how could he stay calm if he hadn't started out calm?

"Slow easy breaths, Moms. Your whole body is relaxed," Fran intoned. "Keep your partners focused, Dads."

Blake raised his hand in an attempt to draw Wren's attention away from his face. If she just wouldn't look at him with those dark Bambi eyes, he could depersonalize the whole scene, could chalk crouching on the floor—held immobile by one small hand, rendered defenseless by one overly imaginative woman—as responding to a universal condition. He could feel sympathetic.

"When she goes into transition, Dads, you may have to hold her face to help her focus."

If she would just let go of his hand, he could feel compassion for the pain of women in childbirth all over the world. He could even admit to a certain grudging respect for couples like these who chose to share the experience.

"Let's try that now, dads. Hold her face for focus. Moms, nice deep breaths . . ."

Try *what?*

Tugging his hand free, he sat back on his heels. This wasn't some abstract universal mother. This was Wren. He *couldn't* cup his hands along her smooth temples, couldn't let his fingers stray into the silk of her hair, to feel the steady thrum of her heartbeat there.

He'd already done that. He couldn't handle that kind of focus.

How could he have let himself get into this?

To his relief, the music stopped, and the overhead lights blazed.

If he hurried, he could get out of here without causing a disturbance. He stood, refusing to make eye contact with Wren. He avoided her questioning gaze.

"Mr. Brockman, you must have a sixth sense. I was just going to ask for a volunteer." Fran took two long-legged steps, positioning herself between him and the door. "We're going to do something a little different tonight."

"I was about to leave." The sight of Fran's fists settling on her narrow hips caused him to reconsider. Her methods of persuasion reminded him a lot of Aunt Ruby.

"Surely you're not going to abandon your partner in the middle of labor." She might as well have added, "Gotcha."

Laughter spread through the room. The dads weren't going to cut him any slack, either.

"Let's show a little courage here, men," Fran goaded. "I need a volunteer."

"Go ahead, Blake," Wren murmured from where she sat on the floor. "Where's your spirit of adventure?"

He knew that poker-faced gaze. She was daring him. "A smart man doesn't volunteer for an unde-fined mission," he muttered. "Only a fool does it *twice.*" Even on the verge of abandoning her, he still relished her teasing.

"No takers? Ms. March, I'll bet *you'd* be willing to be our first volunteer."

Of course she would. Blake knew that even before she grinned.

"Why not?"

"Good. Normally I'd have one of you fathers up here, because if you're going to be a partner, you have to have understanding. Ms. March, we're going to let you experience the joys of motherhood. Sit down, Mr. Brockman. You need this."

Shades of Aunt Ruby—how could he argue? Resigned, he tried to get comfortable on the floor, though he suspected he wouldn't be comfortable anywhere in the room since Fran's smile promised she wasn't through with him yet.

From a cardboard box, she held up a vest that had all the glamour of a baseball catcher's chest guard. "*This*, gentlemen, is an empathy belly. It will give Ms. March the effect of a thirty-pound weight gain—all in one place. After a while, we're going to let you new fathers try it on."

Laughter and groans that were distinctly masculine rose from the ranks. At least Fran was an equal-opportunity tormentor.

Laying the vest aside, she tied a band of fabric tightly around Wren's rib cage. "This is to make it difficult for you to breathe. That can be a problem when you're eight months pregnant."

Blake watched in reluctant fascination as Fran handed Wren a small pillow and demonstrated where to hold it.

"This will put pressure on your bladder, just like that little tyke has a habit of doing when you least expect it."

Fran made a production of lifting the vest and helping Wren into it. "The front is loaded with metal weights so you get the feel of that extra passenger."

Wren patted the round bulge in front and beamed at her laughing audience.

"Your gown, Mom." Fran slipped a bright blue smock over Wren's arms, then turned her so she could close the opening at the back.

The transformation was immediate . . . and realistic. Uneasy as he was, Blake couldn't stop looking at her. She feigned a waddle to the full-length mirror at the side and turned this way and that, posing in stances that filled the room with laughter. She looked pregnant as hell. And beautiful.

"We hear all the time nowadays that you fathers want to be involved," Fran continued. "You want to be true partners. So, Dad here is going to show us how that works."

She was beckoning to him. *"Oh, no.* I'm not—"

"Tonight you are. Come on up and set a good example for all these real dads."

Fran's implacable gaze denied him any excuses. Yielding to her Aunt-Ruby-like tactics, he jacknifed up from the floor and joined Wren at the front, shoving his fists into his pockets.

His sense of foreboding didn't diminish when he saw Wren's happy face. She looked too convincingly pregnant, and her eyes glowed with delectable playfulness.

He should have stayed at the office. He never should have agreed to the Nestlings account.

The instructor circled around them, dropping items of clothing on the floor. "Okay, Wren, time to pick up the house."

Wren shuffled over and tried to bend down. "Unnfff." Pressing her hand to the small of her back, she wailed, "I don't seem to be able to reach them." She was into the performance full tilt.

"Time for hubby to help out." Fran gave Blake a prod in the ribs. "We have an unusually reluctant hubby here tonight."

She didn't know the half of it, he thought grimly, listening to the laughter. Unexpectedly, the sound triggered a memory of a room full of people, of an ill-fated magic act, of everyone laughing . . . except him. And the woman he'd planned to marry leaving . . . with another man.

He would do better this time. At least he wouldn't spoil Wren's fun, wouldn't send *her* packing.

Skulking across the floor, he plucked up the items Fran had dropped, shaking out a man's dark sock with a hole in the heel, a rumpled towel, a pair of extra-large, very flowery boxer shorts. He let his eyes widen with shock.

Wren's delighted laughter mingled with a new outburst from the group, and he found he could laugh with them. The little object lesson hadn't been so bad after all. He'd survived.

He handed the clothing to Fran and turned toward his place on the floor.

"Ve-ry *good,* Dad," she commended, "but don't go 'way yet." She thumped him soundly on the shoulder. "It's time for our hero to take Mom to bed."

Blake choked. Sudden panic gripped him, and he refused to even glance at Wren. Not a heroic reaction, but the situation had swung dangerously out of control.

"You'll need to help little mother, because she's going to have trouble getting comfortable. Here." Fran pelted him with a barrage of pillows, sending the onlookers into gales of laughter.

She was merciless. They were all merciless, enjoying his new predicament and the heat climbing his neck. He was trapped. Nothing to do but play it out.

"Okay, little mother," he said, parroting Fran's words, "let's get you down." He made himself reach for Wren's hand.

She smiled, not the taunting chin-tilted grin he'd expected, but a soft, almost contrite little curl of her lips that weakened his self-control, made applesauce of his knees.

Her hand was warm and receptive and felt small in his... an awareness that roused an ache he'd been trying to ignore. She grasped him tightly, and he felt her accept his support as she lowered herself to the carpet. He felt her trust. It was a new and daunting realization.

"Now the pillows," Fran chimed in. "One for her head, one under that tummy, one between her knees. Help her get settled."

The woman was ruthless. He made a production of plumping the pillows, of choosing the softest first. He knelt down and slid it under Wren's head. Tendrils of satiny hair slipped through his fingers. She smiled at him, held his gaze as if to reassure him, and he had to stop himself from reaching to brush a dark strand from her face.

Laughter brought his head up. Damned if he hadn't become the evening's top entertainment. Worse, he was almost enjoying it. He grimaced woefully at Wren's false tummy and was satisfied to hear another laugh from the crowd.

"You can do it, partner," she whispered.

She looked small and helpless and trusting, waiting for him to take care of her. Squaring his shoulders, he slid his hand gingerly under the false tummy.

It was heavy. Did babies-in-waiting weigh that much? With the least contact possible, he slipped the pillow underneath and withdrew.

Now for the most difficult of all. He forced his gaze lower and discovered that Wren had already wedged a third pillow between her knees.

Relief surged through him. "Whew!" He swiped real sweat from his forehead. The answering laughter was sympathetic.

It was time for this performance to end. "Sleep well, dear," he murmured. Enjoying the merriment that brightened Wren's eyes, he patted her false tummy and shifted to rise.

"The acting was pretty good, Dad, but you just blew your chance for an Oscar." Fran put her hand on his shoulder and held him in place. "At this point, no man in the world says, 'Sleep well, dear.' Am I right, ladies? He says, 'Honey, let's make love tonight.'"

The room exploded with laughter.

Funny. It really *was* funny. Though he would have laughed more easily if some other poor sucker were kneeling where he was. If he didn't have to face the unabashed glee he knew he'd find in Wren's eyes.

But she wasn't laughing. She wasn't even smiling, that full sassy smile he'd expected, full of rich teasing. Instead, she was hugging a pillow, looking downright uncomfortable. And guilty. As red-faced as he.

Sweet and enticing—and pregnant.

And sexy as hell.

He knew then, with gut-wrenching certainty, that Fran was right. He wanted to take Wren home with him. Damn it, he wanted to carry her to his bed. He wanted to make slow fiery love to her. Tonight.

"Thanks to Ms. March and Mr. Brockman for contributing to class. With a little prodding, you two make great partners." Fran winked broadly at Blake. "Those of you who haven't completed an interview, please see them before you leave."

Fran's "little prodding" was about as subtle as a lion trainer with a chair and whip, Blake brooded, but even a subdued lion could roar. Blake couldn't even pace the perimeter of this cage.

Shoving himself up from the floor, he scanned the room, counting four couples waiting to be interviewed. With luck, they might all be out of there in half an hour.

He could be out of there. Away from ballooning mothers and hovering fathers, away from discussions of nursing versus bottles, of cloth versus disposable diapers and the pros and cons of circumcision. The thought made him wince. They were issues he'd never even *thought* about thinking about.

He could be away from Wren. Another issue he didn't want to think about.

A weekend wasn't a lot of time to get his priorities back in order, but that's how he intended to spend every single waking second. He hadn't spent enough time on the airport account, and he needed to start a couple of new proposals.

Since he wouldn't be able to sleep anyhow, he would exhaust his mind with numbers and his body with late hours. So he would stop thinking about her. Stop remembering sweet kisses that made him want more. Stop imagining her in his arms.

The sooner he got started, the better. He strode to the corner where Wren stood holding the clipboards and chatting with several couples.

"Blake, if you want to leave, Jaime and I can finish up here."

That should have sent him on a hasty, and grateful, flight out the door, but instead, her unexpected offer put all his resolutions on hold. She was getting much too good at reading him. And he wasn't about to leave her here with Jaime.

"I didn't stay through the class just to make my acting debut. I want to be sure we have plenty of input from the fathers." Escape into a Colonel mode: *semper fidelis*—always faithful—to his business, maintaining stone walls to protect against butterflies. "Besides, I don't see Jaime here. Let's get busy."

"I hope you're not upset about that little comedy act."

She sounded concerned, but he recognized a sparkle that undermined him all over again. "We weren't Burns and Allen. We could use a little practice." From the widening of her dark eyes, he knew she was as surprised by his answer as he was.

"*I* thought you were great," one of the waiting mothers offered. "I haven't laughed that much in ages. You guys are a good team."

The fact was, he hadn't laughed like that, either, since…he couldn't even remember when. This was the first time in years he'd been more caught up with people than with numbers, more interested in hopes and dreams than in profit margins. More aware of simply being alive.

He and Wren *had* made a good comedy team, but the real teamwork was in the way they were handling the Nestlings project together.

The realization startled him. They *did* work well together.

"Hey, Bird Woman, did I get back in time?"

Blake gritted his teeth.

"Yes, Jaime, but we're almost done."

"Jaime, why don't you—" Blake stopped himself. It wasn't his place to direct the workers on Wren's project. He wasn't the one to send Jaime home. "Why don't you...work here and I'll take that corner."

Jaime looked surprised. "Thanks, Mr. Brockman."

Blake picked up his clipboard and beckoned the nearest couple to follow him. He could still hear Jaime talking from across the room.

"So what do you say, Wren? Have you been promoted to full partner yet?"

Partner? He'd heard the word over and over tonight and never once thought beyond the couples surrounding them.

Full partner? Damn, he'd forgotten about his company shares. Was that what Wren was after, full partnership in his company? Just like the women he'd interviewed, the ones who wanted both worlds.

He finished the questions to his couple without probing for extra answers and bid them good-night. Making a pretense of adding to his notes, he waited until Jaime began the last interview. With Wren free, he marched over to where she waited and handed her his clipboard.

He'd just made a major change in his plans for the weekend, and she needed to know about it.

"If you're ready to go, I'll walk with you to your car. We have some arrangements to make."

"Thanks, Blake, but Jaime drove me." She slid the clipboards into a bulky tote bag, then looked up with a radiance that reached out to him. "You wanted to tell me something?"

What he wanted was to insist she abandon Jaime and ride home with him. What he should do was take control of his impulse, clamp his mouth shut and go directly back to the office to work. Instead, he looked straight down from the ledge he'd climbed out on...and took one step forward.

"I'll be by to pick you up tomorrow morning. Be ready at nine-thirty, and bring your checkbook."

Astonishment didn't even come close to describing the look on her face. "But, Blake, why?"

"I'm taking you to meet some of my shareholders."

Chapter Eight

Snowy mountains skirted both sides of the ribbon of gray highway, and above, an expanse of cloudless cerulean-blue sky stretched away forever. Through the windows of Blake's Rover, Wren saw columns of smoke drifting heavenward, marking the chimneys of winter-hidden homes dotting the sides of the hills. As they sped along the foot of Genesee Mountain, she searched for the oval "spaceship" house high on its crest.

A familiar landmark it was, that house of glass and concrete sparkling under a mantle of pristine snow. It reminded her of days when life had been as simple as passing an algebra test or bluffing a round of poker with the guys at the general store. As predictable as races down the ski slopes after school, porcupine meatballs for supper and two or three kids to look after in the evenings while she did homework and her dad watched boxing on TV.

She glanced over at Blake. He was still ensconced behind aviator sunglasses and a protective shield of grouchiness, as he had been for most of the trip.

Life wasn't quite so simple and predictable anymore. Neither was Blake.

Outside the car, the air was snowflake-crisp and smelled of wood smoke and pine. Beneath them the deep-treaded tires hummed a two-note song. Ahead sugar-powdered peaks promised great skiing and picture-postcard views. A perfect January day.

Wren sighed. It was the kind of day that should stir a man's blood, charge him with energy, fill him with anticipation. It didn't seem to be working for Blake.

"You look like you ate gruel for breakfast, boss."

His response came out somewhere between a growl and a grunt.

"Yep, I was right." She resisted the urge to poke him in the ribs, to throw something at him, to let out a hearty "Yee-haw!" Anything to get him to look at her instead of retreating into that infernal eyes-straight-ahead military grimness he'd assumed from the minute he'd picked her up.

"Now that I observe you more closely, you probably should have stayed in bed."

The crinkling at the corners of his eyes was the only indication he'd even heard. He kept his gaze riveted ahead.

Ahead was exactly what she wished they could talk about...what lay in store for her up the road, at the casino in Central City. Why had Blake insisted he take her to see his shareholders?

When she'd first blurted out her idea of buying more of his shares, he'd behaved as if the likelihood fell right in there with selling her his left arm. He'd obviously hated the suggestion. This morning, his mood made pretty clear that in spite of how well they were working together on the Nestlings account, he hadn't changed his mind. He didn't want her as a partner.

So why the offer to meet his shareholders? More to the point, if he didn't want her as a partner, how smart was she to pursue it?

"Blake?" She leaned toward him, trying to see his eyes. "Would you like to stop for a cup of coffee?"

"No."

She could almost hear him counting to ten.

"We're almost there. I'll get one at the casino."

"Aha! You can speak. I had no idea you were such a cheery morning person."

His head turned a scant degree, but it was enough to betray a reaction. Enough to kick up her heartbeat.

It probably wouldn't be wise to push him, but then lately, with Blake, prudence hadn't been her strong suit. Lately, she'd been downright careless about letting her heart lead.

He'd been so funny and endearing last night, the embarrassed reluctant husband. And he'd looked like he enjoyed her teasing. But then he'd balked, marched right off into that infernal fortress again.

She sighed at his exaggerated concentration as he guided the Rover onto the two-lane road up Clear Creek Canyon. If she couldn't break through his stone wall, she might as well watch the scenery.

Snow stood in high mounds on either side of the road and lay in frozen patches under the tires. The canyon became more winding, and he slowed the vehicle. Her heart gave a little skip of pleasure when she recognized where they were.

"There's a tunnel up ahead, Blake. Toot your horn when we get inside."

He flipped on the headlights, and the car sped into the dark interior. "It's not polite to toot your own horn," he grumbled.

Even in the dim light of the tunnel, she could see he'd screwed his face into furrows and ridges, jutting his chin forward and pursing his mouth. A grumpy face. A deliberate comic scowl. He was mocking himself.

Relief riffled through her. "Darn. Too late." The car sped out of the tunnel into the sunlight. "In tunnels it's okay to toot, Blake. Actually, it's a state law. If there's a kid in the car, you *have* to make echoes in the tunnels. My dad always beeped out 'shave and a haircut.'"

That brought a more obvious look from him, as if he were measuring how serious she was. Would he play along?

"You and your dad were close."

It wasn't a question, yet he seemed to wait for an answer. "You could say that, although he was more like a buddy than a dad. He pretty much left my growing up to me. Look, another tunnel."

Blake reached for the lights. As the Rover raced into the darkness, he tapped out a rhythm on the horn.

"*S-O-S?*" For the first time all morning, Wren laughed. Things were looking better. "There was one thing my dad couldn't abide, though."

"What?"

"He couldn't stand for me to be down in the dumps. He used to bet me that I couldn't stay grumpy for a full count of three." She paused, wavering between letting it go and plunging full-speed ahead.

Damn the torpedoes, she decided. "I'll bet you can't, either."

This time he turned fully to scrutinize her through those awful reflective sunglasses. She couldn't see his eyes, couldn't read if his weather was improving, despite the fact that his eyebrows dipped lower and the corners of his mouth tightened. One thing was certain, though—whether a guise or real, he was fortifying his grouchiness.

"So what were the stakes of your bet?"

"Stakes?" She searched for a plausible answer. "Five dollars." She couldn't tell him they'd always paid off with a big bear hug. It had been part of the game.

"You're on."

"You mean, you want to bet?"

"I never turn down a chance at a fast fiver. A count of three, right?"

"O-kay." She took a deep breath and leaned toward him, taking off her sunglasses so she could look him square in the face.

"Oooonnneee..." She drew the word out, long and slow as her father used to do, letting a smile play across her mouth and dance in her eyes. She searched for Blake's gaze behind the loathsome dark glasses but saw only her own teasing reflection there, distorted as in a fun-house mirror. This might not work if she couldn't see his eyes.

The corners of Blake's mouth tugged downward.

A good sign! "Twwwooo..." she crooned, tilting her head a fraction and deepening her grin.

Blake still didn't smile. In fact, he looked grumpier than ever.

Last chance. This was it. No holds barred. "Thhhhrrrreeee…" She let a chortle warble her voice ever so slightly. In a last ditch effort, she crossed her eyes.

Blake snorted. He coughed. His stony facade crumbled into a broad grin and laughter thrummed from somewhere deep in his chest. With one finger, he drapped the glasses down his nose far enough to look at her over the top. "No fair," he grumbled, a grin overcoming the glare he was trying to recapture. "Anyone would laugh at a face like that."

"Thanks a lot." She grinned back at him. "Five bucks is big money to a mountain-town girl."

"How many times did *you* win?" he challenged. His laughter had spread all the way to his sky-blue eyes.

"Never," she admitted, relishing the throb of his chuckle. She felt a burst of happiness. Things were going to be okay.

"Black Hawk ahead," Blake announced. "We'll be in Central City in a few minutes." He resisted the urge to tap out *S-O-S* on the car horn again, though he knew his raft was in danger of sinking.

He'd *never* been an impulsive person, but impulses were what were getting him into trouble these days. Because of his crazy idea last night, he'd be with Wren today instead of buried in the safe confines of his office. Buried and confined were precisely the way he'd felt when he'd thought about going to the office this morning. For the first time, in a very long time, he hadn't wanted to go to work. That was a dangerous condition.

Impulse had made him insist she meet Roberta and Ernie, because he sure as hell didn't want her going to Kyle Kramer with an offer for his company shares. And that was a concern he needed to give careful scrutiny.

Damnable impulses, keeping him in a constant irascible state. And now he was having trouble with even that. The more he was with Wren, the more he found himself fighting a smile. *Wanting* to laugh.

His raft was in perilous waters.

"Look, Blake. I can't believe how everything has changed since I was a kid."

Nostalgia crept into her voice, giving it a textured huskiness that played havoc with his pulse. He followed her gaze, welcoming the distraction.

A few two-story gingerbread houses still sat at the feet of the enclosing hills, but much of the land had been taken over by casinos, quaint Western-style buildings with names like Bullwhackers and Red Dolly and Bronco Billy's. The old tourist attractions had had face-lifts or had given way altogether to the silvery promises of the gambling industry. And the two-lane highway, even on a snowy Saturday morning in January, was lined with traffic.

"Back then, a cowboy smoked unfiltered cigarettes and scraped cow pie off his boots." Tilting her head, she looked accusingly at his new jeans. "Before going Western was stylish."

"Wearing jeans is hardly a fashion statement," he countered, not bothering to tone down his grin.

"On you they are."

Her eyes were dancing now. With one leg tucked up on the seat, her hair in a thick braid down the back of her sheepskin jacket, she looked a lot like the fifteen-year-old he remembered, the kid she was harking back to. Even at twenty-two, she was still too young. And she wanted kids of her own. Everything about her added up to reasons he had no right to want her.

"I wonder what the town's like now that it's all gambling," she murmured.

She gazed out the window again, and he saw that her teasing had given way to curiosity, her girlishness had mellowed into the quiet anticipation of a woman. He could tell she was looking forward to the day.

So was he.

Maybe they could get through the share thing quickly. He would encourage her to make an offer to Roberta and Ernie; then he'd top it with one of his own. Just to let her know, subtly, that he wasn't going to give up control of his company. He would be very cordial and businesslike, but he'd also put an end to this partnership issue.

Then maybe they could take time for a little fun.

Wren strode down the street beside Blake, hardly hearing the crunch of snow beneath their feet, almost unaware of the cold that bit her cheeks. She was too busy taking in the scene.

Two-and-three-story buildings displayed a solid front of brick and wood along both sides of the narrow street as if they were a set from a Western movie. Except that the buildings here were too pretty, each one adorned with mauve-and-aqua trim or wine-red awnings, pool-hall-green curtains and signs with bright gold letters.

One sign stood out among all the rest, luminous red and green across the front of a large building. Gaming Hall—BUFFALO GALS—Restaurant Bar, it offered in big Western-style letters.

"This is it." Blake stopped before the tall double doors with shiny brass hardware and oval windows intricately etched in flowers. Everything looked spit and polished to a sheen—to lure folks in with their pockets full of silver and high hopes.

She wasn't sure what Blake had planned for her today in this town where everyone came with a dream, but she had a feeling it would take a lot more than high hopes for her to leave a winner.

"Are you ready?"

"I'm ready—" She stopped herself just in time to keep from adding, "Podnah." She didn't want anything to discourage this tentative new camaraderie that played between them like a stumbling puppy.

The moment she stepped through the casino doors, she was sure they'd crossed the threshold into another universe. The scent of fresh popcorn mingled with smoke and a steady jangle of noise, measured whir-thunks and electronic dingle-dingles, and above it all, music. A honky-tonk piano, somewhere in the distance, played a familiar Irish ballad.

A sudden sharp clatter made her catch her breath, halting her in her tracks.

Blake actually laughed. "It's not a raid. Gambling's legal now, remember?" He pointed to a nearby slot machine.

Wren, the small-town girl who'd only gambled in the back of a country store, who'd never heard a one-armed bandit spitting out its payoff, stuffed her hand into her pocket, chagrined. "This is unbelievable."

Blake was unbelievable now that he'd given up his early-morning attitude. Everything added to her overwhelming sense of fantasy.

"Blake!"

Wren turned to see a woman rush down a long curved staircase. Not only was she smiling as if Blake were a long-lost lover, but she was gorgeous: low-cut red dress, a cloud of ruffles bobbing about her knees, deep red hair in a fancy hairdo. Shades of Miss Kitty! They hadn't passed into another universe—they were in Dodge City!

The woman flew into Blake's waiting arms, and right away Wren wished she were packing a six-shooter, or at least that she'd worn something a bit more feminine than jeans and an oversize sweater.

To her astonishment the woman turned and hugged her, too. "Hi, I'm Roberta. And you're Wren. I'm so glad Blake brought you. We never see him anymore."

Wren holstered her imaginary gun and smiled back at Roberta. She liked her already.

Roberta tucked her arm through Wren's. "Just ignore my getup. It's the curse of being the head Buffalo Gal." She cast a disapproving eye on Blake. "When you called, you said she was young, but you failed to mention she was pretty."

Blake's smile took on a tinge of strain around the edges. "It wasn't a social call."

"Nothing is social with that man." Roberta talked as if he weren't there. "Come on. I'll show you around before he makes us get down to business."

Business. Of course. Blake had brought her here for just that, to meet his shareholders, to call her bluff on the threat she'd made to buy more of his company's shares. How ironic to find herself considering one of the biggest gambles of her life in the middle of a gambling casino.

Not the place for faintheartedness. Flashing Blake a brilliant smile, she let Roberta lead her through the first level of the casino. Wren caught fleeting impressions of red brick and warm wood, of burgundy velvet and mauve satin, overridden by bright neon lights reflecting from chrome slot machines driven by white-haired ladies as well as men in plaid shirts.

Blake shrugged out of his jacket and held out his hand. "Here. I don't like to leave gambling debts unpaid." His blue eyes came as close to a twinkle as she'd ever seen.

For a reckless moment it was enough to make her consider collecting the hug that was proper payment for their bet, but she'd surely send him fleeing back into his fortress. Instead, she held out her hand, felt the weight of coins as they fell into her palm. Quarters—no doubt exactly five dollars' worth—and a brief touch that made her breathing falter.

"Let's see if Lady Luck is with you."

So far, she had to be, because Blake's mood was too good to attribute to mere chance or her own fumbling efforts. "I never rely on luck." She squinched her nose to emphasize the claim, then stepped to the nearest machine and dropped in a quarter. A crank of the handle, and she watched the wheels roll to a stop, sending a spatter of coins rattling into the tray.

"See?" She grinned at Blake, then scooped up the quarters.

Blake shook his head. "Beginner's luck." His eyes returned her smile.

"Okay, so now I'm not a beginner." She didn't want this banter to end. Dropping in another quarter, she waited for the wheels to halt. A sharp clatter followed, like rocks dropping into a pot.

"Again!" She turned on Blake. "Dispute *that,* Mr. Naysayer."

He was grinning now. "Nah, these things are set. You just hit one that was due."

"Then you pick one." She loved that he was daring her, loved the unguarded playfulness in his eyes.

"This one." He led her to a giant machine encircled by a frame of blinking lights. Everything about it was exaggerated in size.

"You're on." She studied the options. For three quarters, she could win—or lose—on a variety of combinations. She might as well do it all at once.

She slipped in the coins, then smiled up at him sweetly. "Better see if Roberta has a wheelbarrow." Then she pulled the handle.

Motors hummed, wheels turned, unseen mechanisms clicked and the wheels settled into...jackpot.

"Look."

The second set of wheels stopped on...jackpot.

"Blake!"

She grabbed his arm, holding her breath as the third set of wheels bounced, one after the other, into place. *Jackpot!*

She wasn't sure if the squeal she heard came from her or someone in the gathering crowd. Bells clanged, calliopes whistled and coins hammered into the tray like a hailstorm on a broad tin roof.

For a moment, she thought it was her heart. Through the soft lamb's wool of Blake's royal blue sweater, she could feel his warmth, could detect the flex of his muscles, a sensation that sent a current through her fingertips and made bells peal in her chest.

Bells that echoed into silence as she watched his smile stall, saw the pleasure in his eyes slide into conflict. She followed his daze down . . . to where she held his arm.

Dear God, she'd done it again, reached across his invisible barrier to share her excitement. It was something she did as naturally as breathing. Only, suddenly, looking back to the smoldering in his eyes, she couldn't even draw in a breath.

Quickly she let go, looked away. She couldn't bear to see him retreat into the rock-man role.

"I think the Lady's with you, Wren." Roberta laughed as she scooped quarters into a plastic container. She seemed unaware of Wren's disastrous mistake. "Better look out, Blake," Roberta warned. "Wren's got the touch."

She had the touch all right, Wren thought to herself wryly. A touch that sent the man running from his feelings as if she were still a youngster and forbidden territory. As if the possibility that he might want her threatened to destroy his well-managed world.

Ruby had done a good job of raising Blake, but, damn, he still had some things to learn. A touch didn't have to lead to surrender. A hug wouldn't compromise his control. And a kiss . . . a kiss could lead anywhere that he would let it.

But how was she going to teach him if he kept running away?

Roberta took Wren's arm. "Come on, Lucky. I'll get someone to collect your winnings. Let's go upstairs. You coming, Blake?"

He mumbled an answer, his well-practiced scowl threatening to return.

After all her efforts to draw him out, did they have to go back to square one...*again?* Damn it, she wasn't going to let him get away with that anymore. She linked her other arm through his and smiled up at him, daring him to disengage himself. "Come on, Blake. Tell me what's upstairs."

"The bar," he bit off. His voice was husky, but he didn't pull away again. "More slots." He let her lead him up the burgundy stairs, in step with her and Roberta. On the second floor, he stopped to point at the semicircular tables to the right. "Blackjack." He turned to face her with an unspoken appeal that was half smile, half apology. "And poker in the back."

A cloud seemed to lift and disappear, leaving her heady with promise. Of what, she wasn't certain, but in a fantasy world where Lady Luck played with people's dreams, anything could happen.

Wren's smile felt full of impudence. "Did you say poker, Blake?"

Chapter Nine

"Ernie, you cardsharp, you haven't changed a bit."

"Blake, you old number cruncher, it's good to see you!"

Wren watched in amazement as a solid block of a man charged toward them across the casino's second level. Blake met him halfway, grabbing the man in what looked more like a wrestling attack than a greeting. He thumped the man's back soundly. Was this the Blake Brockman she knew?

"And this must be the little lady who's got the spit and vinegar to stand up to you." Although he stood at least a head shorter than Blake, Ernie moved him aside as if he'd quite finished with him and ambled over to pump her hand.

"Welcome, Wren. We short folks seem to be the only ones who can get Blake to stop counting beans." He grinned into her eyes, and she realized he wasn't much taller than she.

She liked Ernie instantly. How could she not with his white crew cut and his red plaid shirt, his boxer's angled nose and mountain-town orneriness? Ernie Branson could just as well be one of the poker players at the general store back in Antler—bursting with fabrications and colorful stories. As original as homemade beer.

"She does a better job than you ever did, you scruffy critter." Blake joined them, stepping between her and Roberta to rest an arm around each of their shoulders in a startlingly affectionate gesture. "Roberta, I never have understood why you married this character."

Wren felt her heart stumble and break into an erratic sprint. Things were happening too fast. Just minutes ago, Blake had acted as if she'd invaded his private castle, yet now his arm lingered on her shoulder with an ease almost like possession. And mixed with his heckling were words that could go to her head. And her heart. In his eyes she saw a real fondness for Ernie and Roberta.

Ernie's regard for Blake was just as apparent, though she realized as she struggled to regain a semblance of calm that his eyes held more than a little mischief, as well. He looked about as spicy as jalapeño peppers. Wrapping her arm through his, he led her away from Blake. She had to stop herself from refusing to budge.

"Let me tell you, Wren, Roberta's task is nothing compared to what you've survived working for this old reprobate." He winked, then turned to Blake. "Hot damn, Blake, why aren't you *giving* this woman shares in your company? She's real pretty. I'll bet she's smart, too."

She didn't want to see Blake's reaction, not after he'd just recovered from her wayward hand on his arm. This was too much like racing through a mine field, never knowing what disaster she'd encounter next.

So Blake had told Roberta and Ernie she'd come to buy their shares. Maybe she had. She couldn't be sure of anything right now except that she needed to catch her breath, needed to get to safer ground where she didn't overreact to Blake's every change of mood. She needed to stop her heartbeat from skyrocketing.

"What's that they're playing?" She nodded toward three tables in the back, hoping to postpone dealing with the question of the shares. At least for a little while.

Ernie squinted one eye. "Somehow I get the feelin' you're not lookin' for me to answer 'poker.' It's a game called Texas Hold'em. Ever played it, Wren?"

"No, but it looks interesting. Can we watch?"

"Most of them love an audience long as you don't kibitz." Ernie led her nearer.

She wasn't sure if Blake and Roberta followed, and she refused to turn and check. Instead, she let her attention be captured by the players seated at the tables. Almost all of the men wore baseball caps, just like the guys in Antler. It was the gambler's uniform. She felt as if she'd come home.

Out of habit, she sized up the competition. Two of the tables were filled with older men and a couple of women, all leaning back blank-faced and bored, or hunched over the padded mauve edges, squinting at their cards, a cigarette burning to ash in a nearby ashtray. Wistfully, she noted the empty chairs at the third table.

"Hey, girlie, you look like you could give me some luck. Come on over here." A man with coppery whiskers and a red Cardinals baseball cap beckoned from the third table. "You," he answered her questioning look. "Come on, chipmunk, and don't the rest of you just stand there gawkin'. Put your money to work."

She'd been called "Bird Woman" and "mosquito," but never anything as fun as chipmunk. She could almost forgive the old codger for calling her "girlie."

"I'll play with a Card's fan, old-timer." Blake stepped forward. "Deal me in."

"You play poker, Blake?" This was too much to hope for.

"He used to, before he started that infernal business," Ernie complained.

Blake punched Ernie's arm. "That 'infernal' business will make you a pile of honest money one of these days. Come on, Wren. Sit with this fellow and help him win some of the devil's silver."

Excitement sent sparks skipping through her limbs—a sure sign that she should stay glued right where she stood, safe and uninvolved beside Roberta and Ernie. But she'd never been real good at shoulds…any more than her dad had been when he'd taught her how to play at the age of six. Instead, she stepped back into the mine field and dropped into the chair beside the old man.

"Harold's the name." He offered a knobby hand and a grin short a couple of teeth. "Got yourself a pretty one here, young man," he shouted to Blake, who had settled at the end of the table. "Sure you don't want her warmin' your luck?"

Blake leaned his chair back on two legs. "Don't need luck when you've got skill."

She recognized his expression—cordial and closed. Before her very eyes, the businessman had just become the unreadable poker player. He probably played as he did everything else—with intensity, concentrating all that controlled energy on winning.

Suddenly she knew why she was having trouble breathing again. Sitting forward, she listened to the rules, watched Blake peel bills from a money clip and hand them to Ernie in exchange for chips.

"Everyone ante up," the dealer called.

She'd seen enough. "Excuse me, could you wait just a minute?"

The question in Blake's eyes was just what she'd hoped for, and it confirmed what she'd suspected. Even at a poker table, she could see through his wall of control.

"Roberta, do I have credit against my winnings downstairs?" She watched with satisfaction as Blake focused baffled eyes on her.

Roberta nodded.

"Good. Then could someone bring me a beer? And, dealer, would you please deal me in?"

A *beer?* Blake almost blurted the question outright until he saw Wren slip out of her jacket and hang it on the chair next to the old-timer. She tugged down her long black sweater and pushed up the sleeves like a fighter, unaware that the whole operation accentuated her exquisite curves and drew an appreciative audience of retirees. Reminding him that she was of legal drinking age.

She always managed to come up with something unexpected. As usual, he wasn't prepared. Not for his pleasure when he saw her excitement, certainly not for his crazy reaction when she'd grabbed his arm downstairs.

He could understand his response to her last night, could even excuse himself for it. After all, he was a man, and even in that ridiculous empathy tummy, she'd looked small, soft. In need of his help.

But *here,* in the hubbub of a garish casino, just because she put her hand on his arm? Here he had no excuses for wanting to carry her off to his bed, except that she was lovely and tantalizing and...

Off-limits. He could hear the Colonel bark the words. He didn't need the Colonel to tell him he had a company to build, no time for personal pursuits, no right to anything permanent with the kid—the woman—who used to be his ward. Worse, he had no idea how to deal with feelings that led to wedding bells and babies.

He couldn't yield to this attraction. Not with Wren. In the end, they'd both be hurt. He didn't want to hurt her.

The whir of shuffling cards snapped his attention back to the table, to red rectangles sliding across gray felt. He'd better spend all that rampant energy keeping an eye on Wren's undisguised reactions. These old codgers might look up from their cards long enough to admire a winsome figure, but they'd have no qualms about taking advantage of her inexperience.

He glanced at his two cards. They were good enough to stay a round or two, long enough to waylay Wren from any major losses. "I'm in," he declared.

From the look on her face, she must not have much of a hand herself. Her eyes were hidden beneath charcoal lashes, her brow smooth, her full lips pursed in concentration.

At first he didn't understand when the dealer spun three cards into the center and her expression hardly changed. They were good cards...cards a novice should react to. That's when it hit him. She *wasn't* reacting.

"I'll raise."

But she *was* betting. And she'd reduced her expressions to two—serious, and more serious.

How was he going to help her if he couldn't read her? If every time she looked at him, he forgot what he was doing?

The fourth card settled in the middle.

"I'm in," she murmured.

He coughed quietly when she threw in her money, but she seemed to have gone deaf. The fifth card glided to the center, and he stopped short of nudging her under the table.

"I'm out," she said matter-of-factly, sliding her cards to the dealer.

He knew it. She was both inexperienced *and* optimistic—fatal traits in gambling. He'd have to find a way to discourage her from betting.

But he couldn't catch her attention through the entire next hand, and she didn't look up until she won. At the end of the next hand, she raked in the pot and shot him a million-dollar smile.

And her cards hadn't even been all that good.

"Seventh-inning stretch," Ernie announced. "New dealer. Blake ... Wren, can we talk?"

Blake whacked himself mentally on the forehead. Roberta and Ernie needed to get back to work, and there he sat, letting his own game go down the tubes while Wren was doing fine...without help from him. At least Roberta and Ernie remembered why they'd come.

He was surprised when Roberta beckoned him to join her on the brocade love seat near the bar instead of leading them back to the office.

"Game a little off today, Blake?" She bumped him with her shoulder.

"Roberta, what are you up to?" He'd seen her smile like that too many times, and it didn't bode well. Something was afoot when she slanted that coy look at him.

He grabbed a handful of popcorn from the small table and waited impatiently for Ernie to sit next to Wren on the opposite settee. Impatience became annoyance when Ernie rested an arm along the curve of the sofa, including Wren in its circle. Blake shoved fingers back through his hair, irritated even more by the fact that he was irritated.

"Wren, Blake told us you're interested in buying our shares of his company," Ernie began.

At last they were getting down to business. Blake shoveled popcorn into his mouth and fought his agitation, all the while watching Wren. She smiled, a noncommittal smile, and damned if her face wasn't as composed as it had been at the poker table. He'd never seen her so self-possessed. Or so baffling.

"Roberta and I have a proposition," Ernie continued.

Blake shot forward. "Ernie, what are you—?"

"Now, hold on Blake. Hear me out. You know you're numero uno in our book, and we liked Wren the minute we met her. That's why Roberta and I don't want to have to decide between the two of you.

"We'd like to suggest a little game. Make the stakes the right to buy our shares. Leave the decision to skill—"

"And Lady Luck?" Blake interrupted. He didn't believe in luck, but something was sure taking care of Wren today better than he was.

"Would you spell it out a little more, Ernie?" Wren's delicate face didn't alter from her more serious mode.

"Sure. You two go back to the table and play for a set period of time. At the end, the one who has the highest winnings also wins the right to buy our shares." He paused as if to let the idea sink in. "What do you think?"

Blake eased back into the love seat. It might work. It might actually be perfect. "I don't know. How 'bout you, Wren?"

Dark brown eyes sought his, wide and probing, and he realized she hadn't looked at him straight on since they'd started playing poker. There was something different about her now, an almost imperceptible tilt to her head, a tension in her body, an aura of anticipation. Did she think she could beat him?

"I'm game if you are, Blake." She held his gaze as she extended her hand.

"Done." He took her hand and then couldn't let her go, couldn't stop looking at her and the unguarded reactions in her sweet cocoa eyes—misgivings, resolve, the sharp flash of a dare.

"Come on, Blake. Let's get this show on the road." Roberta tugged Wren away. "Quit intimidating Wren."

What had passed between them wasn't intimidation. It was intoxication…and it had flown both ways. He'd seen it in her eyes, the same simmering desire that he experienced every time she touched him, only this time there had been both touch and intensity.

He waited restlessly for the other players to sit before he settled into his place at the end of the table. His agitation heightened when Wren chose the chair at the opposite end. Because he wanted her nearer. Because he knew it was safer to have her farther away.

Ernie pointed to the giant pocket watch on the wall. "One o'clock will mark the last hand. You'll play it out, and that will end the game. You'll each start with twenty-five bucks of chips." Ernie handed Wren a stack while Roberta brought one to Blake.

"Good luck." Roberta patted him on the shoulder. "I have a suspicion you're going to need it."

Blake shook his head. He didn't believe in luck any more than he believed in magic. Or love. They were all illusions. The only things he relied on were skill and a willingness to take a chance now and then.

He'd never dreamed that getting the shares would be this easy. Ernie had come up with a clever idea, an ideal way for him to deter Wren from becoming his partner without opposing her directly.

But he'd have to stop looking at her, or he'd lose his concentration. He'd have to ignore her or he might have to acknowledge a pang of guilt.

Not that he had any reason to feel guilty. She'd agreed to the bet.

Then why didn't he feel elated?

''Everybody in,'' the dealer called.

She was in all right, clear up to her neck. Wren tossed a chip into the center and tried to size up the weather at the other end of the table. She had to be able to watch Blake's eyes. She'd have to keep him believing she didn't know what she was doing until she figured out what she ought to do. Until she decided if she wanted to win.

Blake's chip clinked onto the others in the middle. ''I'm in.'' He leaned forward on the armrest, watching the cards as they fanned out from the dealer's hand. The royal blue of his sweater deepened the blue of his eyes. All he needed were black garters around his sleeves and a mustache, and he'd be a regular high roller—a gamblin' man. She'd have to be careful so her heart didn't sabotage her game.

But it wasn't her heart that reacted when Blake caught his cards. He slid them slowly across the smooth gray felt of the table, sending shivers skimming down her back as if he'd caressed her skin. Lifting the corners of the cards, he peered under, then snapped them down. He raised his gaze to hers.

She blinked, but it didn't help. She couldn't pull away from his unwavering eyes, blue as a robin's egg, or a faraway sea. Steady and challenging.

Hold it. She was supposed to be reading his mind here, not getting caught up in reactions that turned her insides to jelly and made her forget where she was. Dragging her own cards in, she gave them a quick glance and promptly forgot what they were.

He was throwing her off—whether he intended to, she couldn't be sure—but she would have to avoid his eyes and concentrate on body language if she wanted to know what was coming next.

She also had to decide. Without knowing it, he'd provided her a perfect opportunity. But if she won the shares, she might also win a long-term stint as an old maid. When it came to his company, he had a tendency to get a bit...testy.

She made herself focus on the three cards the dealer tossed into the middle, checking that they combined with her two to make a hand she could bet on.

Blake barely glanced at the cards before his gaze settled on her again. Roberta had been wrong—Blake wasn't intimidating. He was thoroughly befuddling, completely enticing, and he looked as if he were enjoying every minute of it. The corners of his mouth curled with the promise of a smile.

"I'm out," he murmured lazily. With studied nonchalance, he pushed his cards toward the dealer, his smile spreading all the way to his eyes.

Darn him. Any other time his wry humor would have captivated her, but she could feel her hackles begin to rise. He reminded her too much of the men at the general store, so confident, so damned assured, even as they tossed in a hand, that in the end they would win. Was every man part laughing-eyed riverboat gambler?

Her reaction was gut level and quick. She called the last bet and watched the remaining hands turn over. Just as she'd expected, her cards were high. She scooped in her winnings.

"Not bad."

Blake's praise chaffed. She'd rather he'd grind out a curse.

Instead he hauled in the next two pots. He'd won them fair and square—she hadn't backed off—but his assurance still nagged at her. She checked their chips. Blake's stacks were a bit taller than hers.

She felt him watching her, catching her in the act of comparing. She knew she shouldn't look up, because when she did, the jangle of the casino fell away to silence, the people disappeared, leaving her and Blake and the tension-filled air that crackled between them. His eyes told her he was enjoying their little skirmish. Cocking a brow, he assured her he was going to win.

He didn't move except to glance at his new cards. When he raised his long lashes, her heart exploded against her ribs because his eyes held the hard luster of lapis. He looked cool and indisputable, and masculine as hell.

That's when she understood. Blake was a gambler, a *real* gambler. Though he'd probably deny it, she'd seen him take chance after chance with his company. He was a rule breaker and a fortune seeker who staked everything he had on his skill and the simple belief that he would win. That was why he'd backed her on the Nestlings account. No wonder he'd captured her heart.

Understanding swept through her like a wash of tears. He was a gambler, but he wasn't willing to risk his heart.

She forced herself to return his challenge, to act as unrattled as a dozing cat, but her heart searched for answers. If she won this wager, what would it do to the trust she'd begun to feel from him? If she lost, would he ever make her a partner by his own choice?

Damn it, damn it, damn it, how had she let herself get into this? She forced herself to pull away from his steady gaze and draw in her two new cards. One look, and she knew she was in trouble. Her cards were terrible. The only way she could win this hand would be to scare everyone off. If she wanted to win, she'd have to bluff big-time. But did she want to win?

"Five till one," Ernie announced. "Last hand."

Be bold, her father had taught her. *Just do it,* Blake had said. Then he'd kissed her.

At her next turn, she bet. Big time.

Blake whistled. Pure folly made her look up. He was impressed, she could tell, but she could feel the sparks, too, traces of fire in his eyes that sent a rush of heat to her cheeks and a swirl of ice through her veins. She was in for the duration now.

The betting jockeyed around the table, and she tracked it with her best poker face. The dealer flipped three cards into the center, and she breathed in slowly to cover her sinking spirits. They were good cards, but combined with her two, they weren't worth a plug nickel. Lady Luck seemed to have taken a powder.

"In for five."

"See you and raise five."

The betting circled the table, and each time, she couldn't bring herself to fold, to throw in a hand that was going nowhere fast.

Two people dropped out, and she wavered between relief and dread. Blake watched her closely.

The fourth card fell, offering her a slim possibility of a hand. Now she couldn't quit. At least not until she knew she *could* win...if she wanted to.

"In for five," she declared and felt the tension mount. Three more people dropped out.

"I'll see your bet." Blake half smiled, looking as confident as the devil himself.

Harold tossed his chips in after Blake's.

A streak of white flew across the table, and the final card slid to a stop. Wren swallowed a groan. She couldn't use it.

She tapped her fingers on the table, then counted chips for a bet. Then counted them again.

And tossed them into the middle. "In for the limit."

That was when she saw it, an almost imperceptible flicker of uncertainty in Blake's eyes.

"I'll see your bet...and bet the limit again." He said the words forcefully.

That was when she knew. He was playing the same game as she. He was bluffing, too.

She should have known. A real gambler didn't give up if there was any chance at all.

She toyed with her chips, letting them drop one by one like the ticking of a clock. Blake's stacks were still a few chips higher than hers.

"You gonna see that bet, or what?"

Harold's question stomped into her gloom, made her draw in a deep breath.

This was it. She had to decide—throw in her cards and give Blake the hand, or call his bluff. *Let* him win, or play to win.

Tears gathered in the back of her throat. Her dad hadn't taught her to play to lose.

"Harold, I'll tell you what. I'll see Blake's raise." She paused at his muted chuckle. "And *double* it." Her words fell into dead silence.

"I'm outta here." Harold tossed his cards to the dealer. "Showdown time." He giggled and rubbed his hands together.

Blake studied her with eyes that had gone as dark and obscure as twilight and made her pulse pound in her ears. His guard was in place again, the walls of his fortress thicker than ever. Would he throw his hand in?

"I'll see your cards, Wren." He tossed his chips into the middle.

He had winning cards after all! She'd lost, fair and square, without giving in. He could have the shares, and she could keep her self-respect. She didn't even care that he was making her own up to it, making her show how badly she'd been bluffing.

Slowly she turned her cards over, cringing visibly as she pushed the ten of hearts forward to match the ten on the table. A miserable pair of tens. She braced for Blake's taunt.

But when his laughter came, there was no humor in it. "You've been betting all this time on a pair of tens?"

She wished desperately she could pull away from the conflict in his eyes.

"You beat me at my own game, Wren." He turned his cards over and shoved forward a pair of eights.

Chapter Ten

A pair of eights. Half a Dead Man's Hand. For once in his life, he should have given at least a passing nod to superstition. Blake tromped into the elevator of the Women and Children's Hospital and stabbed the fourth-floor button.

Never mind that it was more than Wren's reckless eagerness, more than her dark and daring eyes that had caused him to stay in the game so mulishly. Given another chance, he knew he would play the hand the same, all the way to the end of the bungee cord. He had to know what she was betting on. He could no more have thrown in his cards than he could have handed over half of his company to her.

But two damn cards...turned over so slowly he could feel her resistance all the way at the other end of the table. A pathetic pair of tens! As shocked as he still was, he felt the same admiration that had cooled his jets on Saturday.

The kid had guts—far more than he'd given her credit for. She'd won the game fair and square, outplayed him right down to the very last bet with a hand almost as lousy as his.

He couldn't even take consolation from the fact that with two cards like his, Wild Bill Hickok had lost his life. Stubborn Blake Brockman stood to lose his *company*. Maybe that was stretching things a bit, but with Roberta and Ernie's shares, Wren would own a full forty percent, which was almost as bad.

That was another number that had kept him awake nights since he'd driven her back to Aunt Ruby's. The percentage and the haunting image of a dark-haired, dark-eyed woman he shouldn't be calling a kid.

The elevator door slid open, and he stepped into a hallway of rosy wallpaper and wine-and-gray carpet that made him search for an IV pole or a gurney to assure him he was in a hospital.

Another hospital. He must be some kind of glutton for punishment, showing up again to be exposed to dreamy-eyed fat ladies whom he couldn't help but admire at the same time he got reminded once more of all the reasons he should stay away from Wren. He must be getting soft in the head, because he'd found himself watching the time until he could leave the office. If he had his priorities right, he wouldn't even be here, but the bottom line had taken on a curve that had a whole lot more to it than dollars. He wanted to see Wren.

"Over here, Mr. Brockman."

Of course, Jaime Sandoval would always show up. Blake spotted him near the circular nursing station with three of his other part-time employees. And

Wren. Jaime stood so near to her, they might as well have been handcuffed.

Jaime was becoming predictable. But there was no evidence of the daring-eyed gambler with the pigtail who'd stood up to Blake on Saturday. Wren looked as muted as her butterscotch business suit, and her smile held all the warmth of a ray of fluorescent sun.

"We were just dividing into teams," she announced. "I think that will work better for interviewing couples."

She was the epitome of poise, a picture of control. The bird's-nest pin on her lapel caught his eye, shot him back to the morning she'd made the presentation to the Nestlings people. She'd taken control then, too, and had rocked the very floor under his feet with her radiant charm. But something was different today.

His steps slowed as he tried to fathom her change. It came to him in a rush. Her glow was gone.

That put him back up to full speed. "Fine. I'll work with you," he announced, joining the group.

Without abdicating, Jaime saluted and put space between him and Wren, leaving Blake feeling both old and mean-spirited.

"If you're ready, I'll take you to see the new mothers." A nurse left the circular station to lead them down the hallway.

Blake hung back from the rest of the group, where he could kick himself without an audience. Because he deserved a good solid boot in the keister for his knee-jerk reaction every time he saw Jaime with Wren.

Jaime was a good employee, a hard worker, putting himself through school, if he remembered right. Not so bad looking that he wouldn't contribute favorably to the gene pool he seemed so intent on creating with Wren. The kind of young man a guardian might well seek for a ward.

That was what he should be doing, finding a mate for Wren, seeing her settled down and starting the family she wanted.

So she wouldn't be so hell-bent on being his partner, he concluded, knowing full well there was another, more relevant, reason. Because he wanted her himself. But not as a partner.

Given the circumstances, he wasn't going to refine his priorities much more than that today. Stepping up his pace, he caught Wren halfway down the hall. "I seem to be spending more time in hospitals nowadays than most doctors."

The brightening he'd hoped for didn't materialize. Instead, her gaze was steady and cordial, her dark eyes the color of old rust.

"I thought you'd never want to see another nurse after Fran."

He chuckled, hoping that laughter really was infectious. "I suppose Fran and storks are necessary evils."

That brought a flicker of surprise to her face, but before he could press his advantage, the nurse pointed them to an open doorway.

Wren stepped ahead of him into an inviting room that looked like someone's bedroom. The floral window treatments and pale peach walls didn't look like part of a medical facility. The bed, on the other hand, did. One young woman was all it would hold on its narrow white-sheeted mattress, and she sat, regulation dishwater-gray gown in place, propped against the raised back. Even the nearby rocking chair, holding a young man cradling a baby, failed to compensate for the institutional bed.

"...and that's our new daughter, Katie." The woman smiled down at the tiny bundle in her husband's arms.

"She's beautiful."

Wren sounded as if she were talking in a library—or a museum—instead of staring at a red-faced wrinkled little prune of a thing trussed up in a flannel sleeper with ducks all over it. She sounded subdued.

But apparently the father missed what Blake had heard. "We think so, too." He beamed up at Wren.

"When will you be able to take her home?" she asked, and Blake expected to hear, "Please respond at the beep." He'd heard computerized telephone surveys with more animation.

"She was born this morning, *very early*. We have to check out first thing tomorrow."

"That soon?"

He detected a spark of interest then, was relieved to see Wren move closer and touch fingertips to the baby's blanket.

"Are you ready?" she asked the mother, never taking her eyes from the baby's face.

"Oh, yes." The mother's voice rang with the eagerness he missed in Wren's. "We've had her room fixed up for weeks."

"But are *you* ready?" Blake raised questioning brows to the father and then wished he could grab back the words. He hadn't meant to get involved, but something was wrong with this scene. Something was missing, but *that* wasn't the question to improve the situation. He didn't think he wanted to hear the man's answer.

"My wife's ready, but I know where you're coming from," the man said. "Sometimes I get real nervous, you know? Like, what do I know about raising kids? Especially a girl!'' His pride hadn't faded, but doubt had crept into his voice.

A nod was all Blake could manage. He did know.

''Were you raised by a single parent?''

Wren's quiet question caught Blake off guard, because she stole the words right out of his head.

''Hell, no.'' The man cringed and glanced at the baby. '''Scuse me. See what I mean? Got to start watching my language. No, my folks raised me and three brothers and one sister. But it's real different when she's your own. You don't want to make any mistakes.'' He looked down at the little bundle and stroked a thumb down her cheek. ''I don't even know what all the mistakes are. I'm not sure I know how to be a father.''

A guy who'd grown up with two full-time parents and a whole raft of siblings didn't know how to be a father? The man's confession didn't help settle an uneasiness in the pit of Blake's stomach.

''You'll be *fine*,'' his wife reassured. ''We're in this together, honey. We'll help each other through the rough spots.''

The knot in Blake's stomach tugged a little tighter. The woman had given the perfect cue for Wren to toss out that ill-fated word, a word he didn't want to hear again. He didn't even want to *think* about partners, knowing that with Roberta and Ernie's shares, Wren would own as much of his company as he did.

But only on paper. As long as she didn't know about Kyle Kramer's shares, as long as he could direct Kyle's vote, he would keep control of his company.

"Hey, would you like to hold her?" The young man leaned forward and offered his baby daughter for Blake's approval.

Wren's chin rose no more than a fraction, a not-quite-disguised hint of envy, but Blake felt it all the way to his toes. "Thanks, but we don't have a lot of time. Do you mind if we ask you a couple of questions?"

The man looked at Wren, and Blake saw it in her eyes when she considered asking to hold the baby herself. Instead, she flipped a page on her clipboard and uncapped her pen. Her already muted sunshine seemed to fade even more.

That was when he understood what was wrong. Her excitement was gone. Almost overnight, she'd become the consummate professional, the committed worker, a woman with the pride—and the pressures—of ownership. She was taking this partnership business to heart. He should have known.

"Fire away," the father answered.

Blake waited for Wren to ask the first question, wondering if the sadness he saw in her eyes was real, or if guilt was what made him read it there.

"You're good at this, you know." Every time he worked a new location with Wren, he had to acknowledge how good she was becoming. Even today, with her chatty openness all but nonexistent, he could see that she put people at ease, she drew them out with a naturalness that made them feel clever and insightful, as if they'd given her exactly what she'd come looking for.

"They say it takes's a good boss to tap an employee's strengths." She proffered a professional smile.

He stopped her right then and there, came around and stood in front of her in the middle of the hall so she wouldn't sidestep and glide coolly away. "Wren March, you sound like you're sucking up."

"I'm *not!*"

He was as shocked at the accusation as she, but it was worth it to see her head snap up, to find indignation spark life back into her eyes. "Can't handle the risk of beating a man at his own game?"

Indignation gave way to pure astonishment, followed by a flash of protest. "I've beaten lots of men at poker, but they didn't sign the paycheck."

Blake's relief threatened to make him take her into his arms. "The paychecks come from projects like Nestlings, and you've done a much better job on that than I have."

He could see her battling between the always-bubbling Wren he knew and the stranger she was trying to be, which made him itch to shake her. Or better yet, to kiss her. But he forced himself to give her time.

Her chin hitched down a notch, and she almost looked relieved. "You're right. I have. But all you have to do is take a few more risks yourself."

He considered the trace of challenge in her eyes, the smile that almost touched her lips. "Like holding that baby?" His question was another of those out-of-the-blue things that startled him even more than her.

Her eyes widened.

"That little creature looked like a bundle of bubbles just waiting for a man in a business suit to come along to let loose on."

He let himself enjoy her tentative smile. "And so many ducks. That child is liable to imprint on her nightie."

A soft chuckle rewarded his efforts.

"But you're right, a few extra minutes to hold the baby would have put the parents at ease. Though, one look at me and she would have started yowling." He could tell she was tickled now.

"At one day old, I don't think they can see all that well, Blake. She wouldn't have known what an ogre you are."

He didn't even see the nurse until she came up to them and cleared her throat.

"Ms. March, the rest of your group went back to your office. Would you and Mr. Brockman like to visit our birthing area before you go?"

He could see Wren's pupils widen, and he imagined he could feel a wave of excitement emanate from her. But then it waned.

"Thanks, but we already have a lot of good information from your new parents."

She was being gracious again, but impassively professional. Not the Wren he wanted to see.

"I need to get back to the computers, and I'm sure Mr. Brockman has things waiting for him, too."

He did. If he had a shred of sense, he would leave right now and let her play this thing through until she came to her senses. Until she stopped impersonating the confirmed curmudgeonly businessman, stopped trying to stack up as a partner. Until she stopped acting like *him*.

"If it won't take long, I think we can risk it." He was an idiot. He was too easy. He couldn't stand to see her that way.

He watched a flurry of emotions change her eyes, like clouds racing across high-speed film: a flash of triumph that cost her some effort to subdue, pleasure that she collected into the poised anticipation of a woman. And something more, something that disappeared before he could name it.

"Good idea," Wren finally answered.

The soft roughness of suede textured her voice, betraying her feelings. It made him feel generous and understanding, as if he'd given her what she'd wanted. He realized with a jolt that he wanted to give her more.

"The families you interviewed before were in our postpartum rooms." The nurse led the way down another hall, oblivious to what passed between them. "This corridor has our LDR rooms. Labor, delivery and recovery," she clarified, smiling at Blake as if he were an alien.

She led them into what looked like another bedroom. "The mother stays here until about two hours after delivery. If labor is long, father can stay with her on a cot. Of course, he's here for the birth, too."

The nurse pointed to the bed with a batonlike device. "The beds adjust for delivery, and they all have stirrups and lighting." She waved the baton toward the ceiling, and two spotlights came on and focused on the center of the bed.

Blake felt himself blanch.

"The mothers are hooked to a fetal monitor throughout labor. Each room's screen shows the entire ward."

For the first time, he noticed the monitor in the corner cabinet, its glowing green window filled with rectangles of ascending and descending lines.

"After delivery, we put the baby here...in the warmer." She pushed aside an accordion wall to reveal another part of the room.

"That's a baby warmer?" Blake studied the plastic contraption that looked more like kin to a grocery cart than to an oven. The hood appeared to be wired for heat and light—and quite possibly CDs and video.

The nurse nodded. "The baby stays in the room with the parents for forty-five minutes before we take her to the—"

A face popped through the door. "Nancy, we've got a mom on the way up. Fully dilated. Baby's almost here."

"Gotta run, folks."

"Thanks for everything," Wren called after the two women.

She glanced around the room, and Blake saw her memorizing every detail, the pastoral painting above the bed, the large plant in the corner. Her eyes kept straying to the baby warmer.

"Oh, dear, are you two still in here? I'm afraid you'll have to leave." The nurse charged back in and herded them out the door.

Wren scurried ahead of him, turning to peer over her shoulder until a flurry of activity in the hall drew her attention. Rolling toward them on a cart came a mountain of a woman, her legs poking up under a sheet like a grasshopper's. She was moaning. Two women in aqua scrubs pushed her along, followed by a man in a ski jacket. Cart, mother-to-be, nurses and father all disappeared into the room.

"That was close." Blake allowed himself a quiet sigh of relief. He'd gotten through a lot of challenges with the Nestlings account, but a baby delivery was not on the agenda.

"Blake, listen."

"Come on, honey, breathe with me. Good. Count my fingers." The husband's anxious voice eddied out of the room to them.

Blake's own breathing stopped, not because of what he heard, but because he saw Wren raise a hand to grasp his arm, then pause, catching herself in mid-motion. She forced her hand back to her side and her eyes away from his.

She might as well have shot him, the pain was that quick, that deep. He'd managed to run the spontaneity and excitement right out of her just when he was beginning to understand that he needed them. He fought to keep from grabbing her and folding her into his arms.

"We'd better go," she murmured.

"Not yet. Listen." He took her arm, turned her back toward the partially open doorway, fought the slow heat that crawled through him.

"That's it, Brenda, look at me. Push."

He imagined the worried man standing over his wife, taking her face in his hands as the birthing-class teacher had shown them. He could actually hear the woman breathing, making throaty sounds that sent a shiver snaking down his back. Only to be wiped out by his awareness of Wren's guarded interest and his own pulse pounding in his ears.

"You're doing great, honey. I can see it. The baby's coming!"

"Blake..." Wren caught his hand then and held on so tight, he was afraid he'd hurt her with his answering grip. She was imagining herself in the woman's place, he knew, just as she had at the birthing class. Anticipation, fear, wonder—he could see her working to keep them from her eyes.

"That's it . . . that's it. One more time . . ."

A sturdy high-pitched cry pierced the waiting air, paused as if to consider the situation, then launched into a full-blown wail. The proclamation of a strong new life.

"I think they'd better get that little one into the bun warmer."

She laughed then, a reluctant laugh, and he discovered that he wanted to smile, too, a really silly grin at this hearty protest to being thrust into the world. At Wren's hand in his. At her barely restrained delight.

Her ebony eyes had come alive again, and flecks of light glittered in what looked like gathering tears. Her hand relaxed into a soft curl in his.

For the first time in his entire thirty-one years, he knew he was in danger of losing it . . . of losing his heart to a little slip of a woman with tears in her eyes. Tears that he wanted to kiss away.

"Two kids gone, seven to go," Ruby announced as she hurried back into the living room.

Wren looked up from the floor where she sat cross-legged with Jaime, six children and an explosion of blocks, plastic dinosaurs and miniature metal vehicles. "How's the snow?"

Ruby settled down with a little girl and a fuzzy purple dinosaur. "It's pretty steady. I hope the other mothers aren't having too much trouble."

The grandfather clock on the mantle read four-thirty—perfect timing for the snow to create chaos out of the already slow rush-hour traffic. Hard to tell how long it would take Ruby's friends to get there to pick up their children. Correction: Ruby's friends' *daughters*.

She reached over to help Jaime and the children add blocks to the tops of several growing towers. "I hope Lisle Mason appreciates this little bonus project you created, Ruby."

Freebie would be more accurate, Wren decided. She couldn't very well charge Mr. Mason for an afternoon of baby-sitting in exchange for in-depth interviews with nine young mothers. She also hadn't had the heart to say no when Ruby had told her of her arrangements.

"Look out . . . look *out!*" Jaime exclaimed.

The towers teetered with promise just before two giggling toddlers clobbered them gleefully. Blocks flew in every direction.

Even the children's laughter wasn't enough to dispel her concern over Blake's abrupt departure from the hospital and his unexpected trip out of town. Blake rarely went out of town.

The doorbell rang again, and Ruby pushed up from the floor. Moments later she returned with four mothers who hugged their charges and led them off to find snowsuits and boots.

"Come on, Nick and Ryan," Jaime said, "let's pick up these blocks. Wren, I'll stick around until all the mothers come."

"Ruby and I can handle two—"

Another chime of the doorbell brought both little boys's heads up.

"You mean three," Jaime corrected. "That doorbell's going to wake Maddie any minute." He glanced toward the dining room, where the seven-month-old baby slept in her portable crib. "When she wakes up, I'll take care of her. She's a sweetheart. Reminds me of you."

Jaime's smile conveyed more meaning than Wren wanted to deal with. She was glad when Ruby and another woman appeared in the entryway to collect the five-year-old, Nick.

"Okay, Ryan, let's build a *real* big one." Jaime helped the towheaded child start another tower. "I'd say you've been doing some pretty good building yourself, Bird Woman. Was the client happy with the results from the day-care center?"

"He said he was very pleased with all our reports."

"What'd the rock-man have to say?"

"I think he's been . . . satisfied."

"Satisfied?" Again there was more in Jaime's inquiring glance than in his words.

"I'd say *very* satisfied," she shot back.

She was pretty sure Blake considered her a valued employee. But there was more. He didn't talk to her like a patronizing big brother anymore, didn't scowl with impatience. He'd even told her she was good.

And he'd kissed her, more than once. With more than friendly persuasion.

But, though he'd reached out to her at the hospital, he'd fled back into his fortress. Worse than that, he'd fled town.

She may have won a battle at the Buffalo Gals casino, but she wouldn't bet a wooden nickel on the outcome of the war.

A clamor of bells and tones interrupted her plummeting feelings.

"I'll get the phone," Ruby called. "You get the door."

Wren hurried to the entryway, hoping that both of the lost mothers had made it through traffic by now. She tugged open the door.

"Blake!" At the sight of him, she almost pushed the door closed. The two days since she'd seen him seemed more like a year. It was all she could do to keep from hugging him. "What are you doing here?"

Snow flecked his hair and the broad shoulders of his camel coat, and cold ruddied his cheeks. The familiar toffee-colored swatch of hair had fallen forward with dampness, but not enough to shadow the unrest in his eyes. A discovery that made her soaring heart stall.

"Ruby said you were stranded with a house full of kids. She sounded like you could use some help."

He seemed concerned, but she sensed an underlying agitation. "Ruby called you? Blake, we didn't need—"

"Blake! Thank goodness you're here. Come in, come in." Ruby dashed into the entryway and plunged into the closet. Emerging with her purple parka and Jaime's jacket, she stuck her head into the living room. "Jaime, come here."

Wren eyed Ruby suspiciously. "What are you doing?"

"Hold this for me, dear." Ruby handed Blake her parka and smiled up at him sweetly, ignoring both their frowns while she bustled into its purple sleeves. "The children's mothers called," she said, occupying herself with the fingers of her leather gloves. "They're stuck in traffic, but they'll be here as soon as possible."

Jaime appeared in the archway with Ryan tagging behind. "What's up?"

"Here." Ruby shoved his coat at him. "I have t'ai chi class and Blake's here to help, so we can leave now. Come on." She grabbed the sleeve of his sweater and all but yanked him out the door. "I'll be home later,

dear," she called as she hauled Jaime down the drive-
way.

"I don't even believe your aunt." Wren closed the
door slowly, delaying the moment when she had to
face Blake's displeasure. "You don't have to stay. I've
cared for half a dozen kids before. Contrary to the
hordes of wild creatures Ruby implied, there's just
Ryan and Maddie, and we'll do fine."

She braced for his tempest, but when she looked up,
he was wavering between what looked like indecision
and amusement.

"My aunt has never been one for discretion." He
sidestepped toward the door, then stopped.

Wren nodded. "I have a tendency to forget that at
the worst times."

Still half frowning, Blake searched her face, then
glanced beyond. "Hey, Ryan."

She'd all but forgotten the little boy. "You'd better
get going, Blake. You'll be forever in traffic. Come on,
Ryan. Let's go play."

Instead of taking her outstretched hand, Ryan
passed her by to wrap his chubby fist around Blake's
little finger. "You come, too."

Just then an undeniable whimper rose in the distance.

Chapter Eleven

"I'll stick around." Blake knew Wren would be surprised at his offer. He was too, but it was her flash of unguarded elation that made him clarify, "Till you take care of the baby."

She glanced back at him, her smile ambivalent. "Thanks, Blake. I think, at this point, a dry diaper is the key to her happiness." She disappeared from the entryway, leaving behind a faint scent of flowers.

She was much too tempting—he'd known she would be. Muted business suit or sexy sweater, talking to new parents at the hospital or making the best of Ruby's schemes at home...it didn't matter. Everything about her made him want her. Which was why he'd stayed away. And the reason he should leave now.

Instead, he coaxed his finger from Ryan's moist grip long enough to shed his coat and stamp the snow from his feet before letting the blond-headed little moppet lead him into the living room. He could hear the baby's cries gaining volume in the dining room, could almost feel the soft comfort of Wren's cooing answers. Sounds that had no business making him smile.

Hunkering down to where he could talk, man-to-man, he looked Ryan in the eye. "Okay, guy. How about cars?"

"Okay. Me want po-weese cah."

"You got it." Blake stretched his long frame on the floor beside the boy and began to sort through the collection of small vehicles—a race car, a jeep, a green truck with doors that he knew would open.

"Hey, look at this!" As he handled each car, he realized he recognized them all.

"What?" Wren popped her head around the archway. Against her shoulder lay a head of straight black hair, and her arm curled around a bundle bigger than the one he'd turned away from at the hospital. The cries from the bundle seemed to be diminishing.

"These are my old cars. I can't imagine why Ruby would have saved them all these years."

"Maybe she's hoping to be a grand-aunt."

"You think so?" The thought had never occurred to him. Before he could see if she was serious, Wren disappeared into the dining room. He could still hear her gentle chatter to the baby, a kind of music he'd be better off ignoring.

"Here we go, Ryan. Vrooom, vroom." He drove the green truck along the curved patterns of the Oriental rug, unable to keep from grinning at the excellent siren sounds pursuing him.

Suddenly it came to him as if it were yesterday. "You know, I'll bet I've driven these carpet patterns a thousand times," he called to Wren.

She appeared in the archway again, holding a bottle in the baby's mouth, head tilted, waiting to hear more.

"I remember lots of winter evenings just like this one. Ruby actually crawled around on the floor with me. The grand piano was a giant parking garage, and—" he paused, trying to remember "—and the bad guys always hung out right behind that chair over there."

"Looks like they're still hiding there." She nodded at him to look at the little boy driving his black-and-white car up the leg of the chair.

The boy reminded him so much of himself. Watching, he felt nostalgia sweep him like a flash flood. So many memories of play, of stories, of make-believe...of all the fun and laughter, and mischief, of growing up in Aunt Ruby's home. He found himself hoping that Ryan's foster home was as happy.

A heart-rending wail brought both their vehicles to a halt, and he looked up just in time to see Wren glide by the archway between the two rooms. Just as quickly, she disappeared, but the baby's cries didn't fade. If anything, the lusty wails seemed to gather strength.

He drove his green truck across the carpet to a vantage point where he could watch Wren. With the baby on her shoulder, she waltzed around the table, swaying rhythmically, murmuring soft soothing sounds.

"Shh. Don't cry, Maddie. Your mama will be here soon," she crooned. With her free hand, she stroked damp tufts of hair back from the baby's red face.

It was a gesture so full of gentleness, Blake felt his guard all but crumble. Mesmerized, he watched her tilt her head to look into the baby's face, her eyes soft as a doe's, her long silken hair swaying forward to mingle with darker feathery wisps. Her luminous face hid nothing of her feelings—concern, sympathy, love. And a deep soul-stirring longing.

He'd never seen anything so beautiful in his life.

She was meant to have children of her own. And he wanted to watch her love them.

The impact of his thoughts caught him right in the solar plexus, all but punching the wind right out of him. What he was feeling went beyond the requirements of a guardian, way past the responsibilities of a boss. Beyond even the carefully banked desire to make love to her.

"Don't cry, Maddie," Wren soothed, provoking a wave of fresh sobs that sounded like the baby's tiny heart was breaking.

The worry on Wren's face was about the limit of what he could stand. He shoved up from the floor. "Can I help?"

Her eyes didn't leave the baby's face. "Not unless you look like her daddy. She's dry, and she'd had some juice. I think she just decided she's had enough of strangers."

"Maybe a new face would . . . kind of distract her."

At that, Wren's head came up. "You're volunteering to hold her?"

"I think so. If you'll show me how."

The tenderness in her eyes was all he needed to make him step nearer, to reach out his arms. If only there'd be a way to capture that look, that breathlessness, the hopeful little smile that told him she was pleased.

"You don't have to be shown. You'll know." She hitched the baby over to him, sliding Maddie into his cradling arm so that he could look down at her puckered red face.

"Maddie, this is Blake," she purred, wiping tears from the baby's cheeks with a slender finger. "I think you're going to like him."

He felt Maddie's little body shudder against him, heard her hiccuping sobs and knew his heart was experiencing major body damage.

"You're holding her just right. All you have to do is walk with her. Sometimes movement will put them to sleep. I'll entertain Ryan."

He wanted to blurt out, "Don't go," but restraint that was too much habit overrode his impulse. He began to walk slowly, carefully, holding Maddie as if he cradled a blanket full of Ruby's crystal goblets. While he moved, he discovered a natural rhythm, as if rocking a baby were an inborn skill just waiting to be awakened by tiny sobs.

And that smell... Baby powder? Dried milk? An overheated little body and sweet salty tears. He drew in a long breath, recognizing a memory, not of anything he could picture in his mind, but of a feeling, a sense of well-being, an assurance of love.

The kind of feeling Wren would give her children.

He didn't even try to stop himself from watching her where she sat building block tunnels for Ryan's cars. As if she felt his gaze, she smiled up at him, a wistful smile that nudged another memory, that brought forth a melody when he hadn't known there was music in him.

A song drifted into sound from somewhere long ago, and he hummed in time to his steps, feeling the deep thrum from his diaphragm against the warm little papoose that was Maddie. The sound made her pause in her miseries.

Were there words? he wondered. Swaying still more easily, he let his mind float. "Don't cry, little donkey, come fly away with me," he sang softly to the little girl, groping for the images Ruby had sung to him so many years ago. "We have wondrous dreams to seek, and time to sip some tea." All from a memory that had been buried so many years, and might have stayed buried except for this little bit of fluff in his arms.

Maddie looked up at him expectantly.

"I don't know what it means, little one."

As if he'd let her down, she gave forth a howl that convinced him she was anything but fluff. What was worse, she looked as if she were winding up all over again.

And Wren was watching. Heaven help him, he didn't want to let her down. Digging into his pocket, he tugged out his keys and held them up before the infant. "Look, pretty Maddie." To his relief, the jingle caught her attention.

Rocking and humming, he shook the keys in front of her, watching her big blue eyes follow them, feeling her trembling sobs subside. From the folds of her blanket, her fat little fist emerged and reached up. He watched in fascination as she touched the keys, smacked her fist against them to make them dance. He could feel the intensity of her concentration as she opened her hand and grasped the largest key. The shiny silver memento—his talisman against illusion. Then she smiled, and his heart turned to silly putty.

"I see she likes your special key," Wren murmured from her place on the floor. "There must be magic in it."

Magic? The key was to remind him there *was* no magic. But there was sorcery in Wren's soft smile and enchantment in Maddie's flailing delight, intoxication in the scent of baby powder and flowers.

"I think maybe, after all, there is."

The key to his heart. Wren mulled the idea as she hurried back from the front door where she'd just sent Maddie off with her mother. Wouldn't it be nice if love could be that simple?

She stood at the entrance to the living room and watched Blake and Ryan. "You look right at home down there." Blake had fallen into a world of make-believe with the little boy as naturally as he'd fallen into charming Maddie.

"This was home for a long time," he answered.

She was glad there was no bitterness in his voice, only the sound of fond memories. More than anything else, this was the kind of home, the kind of partnership she wanted with Blake. But how could she let herself dream such things when he didn't even want her as a business partner?

"Come on, Wren. Our tunnels need some repair," he called.

She plopped down beside them, refusing to look at the clock on the mantel. Blake had forgotten his condition to stay only until Maddie was quieted. If he didn't remember beforehand, she knew as soon as Ryan's foster mother arrived, he'd be out of there. Whatever amount of time he stayed, she intended to enjoy every minute. This might be her one chance to be a family with him.

"Rrrmmm, rrrmmm, come the 'ment truck." Ryan crawled along the floor, pushing a red-and-white truck to the pile of blocks.

"'Ment truck?" she asked.

"*You* know, to cement up the tunnels."

She mouthed the word *Oh.* "I knew that. But what I've never been able to figure out is how come boys can make so much better sound effects than girls. *Listen* to him, and he's not even three!"

"I think it's one of those gender differences."

She was pretty sure he hadn't meant to be provocative, but she couldn't stop a rush of heat from racing through her, couldn't keep her gaze from slipping to his mouth.

"I think I'd better turn on another light." She jumped up and snapped on the table lamp near the front window, filling the corner of the room with a golden glow.

"We need tunnels here, lady, so we can toot our horns."

She reached for the blocks, and Blake's hand brushed hers, sending a swell of gooseflesh whispering up her arm. Now it was her turn to send out distress signals in tunnels. Willing her hands not to shake, she tried to concentrate on restacking the blocks, but in the changing light of the room, she saw Blake's eyes deepen to the color of old glass.

So many times she'd dreamed of evenings like this, stretched out on the floor with Blake and their children, playing and laughing, teasing and touching until they tucked their little ones in . . . and turned to a different kind of play.

"Rrrrmmm, rrrmmm." Ryan drove his toy car up the side of her leg and down the length of her jeans, exiting by route of her shoe. She could feel Blake's eyes following. This wasn't one of those evenings she'd dreamed of, she reminded herself. This was sweetness tinged with sadness, and her imagination was out of control.

Sitting up straighter, she added more blocks to the tunnels and watched Ryan move to Blake. He crawled into Blake's lap, settling in as if he'd sat there a hundred times, leaning his head back against Blake's chest. He rolled the police car lazily back and forth along the arm that Blake had instinctively folded around his plump middle. Ryan's eyes fluttered and he fought to keep them open.

Wren wondered how she could sit there so calmly without overflowing with love . . . for the tired tousle-haired child who curled so trustingly in Blake's arms, for this man so like him, his hair almost as ruffled, who held him so naturally. She'd yearned to know Blake's passion, but his tenderness made her want him even more. She'd never dared imagine him cherishing as he had with Maddie and Ryan.

If she could only reach through the last ragged stones of his defenses, what they might discover together would be like a wild spring storm—full of power and magnificence, spending itself into a slow warm rain followed by sunshine. Maybe even a rainbow.

The thought sent a shiver through her that came to an abrupt stop with the chiming of the doorbell. It sounded too much like the last stroke of twelve, because she knew the fantasy was about to come to an end.

"Ryan, I think that's Sue."

Ryan's bottom lip trembled.

Reluctantly, she rose to go to the door. He couldn't know how much she shared his feelings. Especially when Blake rounded the corner of the entryway with Ryan high on his shoulders, gripping fistfuls of his mussed hair. Blake grinned and then grimaced.

And Ryan giggled, at the same time that crocodile tears traced paths down his cheeks—sheer childish delight mingled with a broken heart because he had to leave.

"I know, Ryan." She patted his arm. "I don't want it to end, either." This time with Blake and the children had been precious.

Ryan's foster mother stood on the doorstep. The woman looked stressed and far too pregnant to be chancing winter traffic jams.

"Sue, I'm glad you're safe. You shouldn't be out in weather like this."

"I'm sorry I'm so late. Traffic is a mess, but we don't have far to go now. I can't thank you enough for watching Ryan." She helped him into his puffy down jacket while Wren stuffed one small foot into a white moon-walker boot and Blake did the other.

"He was great. We had fun, didn't we, buddy?" Blake tied the strings of Ryan's hood, then pretended to steal his nose between two fingers. Ryan giggled. Blake grinned.

"I'm so glad," Sue said. She turned away from the child. "He goes back to his mother on Saturday," she murmured. "She got a job and a place of her own. Can you say thank-you, Ryan?" She nudged him forward.

Ryan didn't need more encouragement to wrap his arms around Blake's knees. "Tank oo, Dada."

"Oh, honey, Mr. Brockman isn't—"

Blake nodded. "It's okay. I don't mind." He knelt and tapped a fist to his chin. "Time to go, tiger."

For the first time, Wren saw the longing in Blake's eyes, saw him wish for more. Faced with one needful little boy and one spontaneous ragamuffin hug, Blake had revealed what she'd known about him all along. He guarded an unfathomable well of love.

But then he stood. Pulled open the door. Smiled at Sue, that inscrutable Brockman smile that never wavered for long, even in the face of gale forces—even in the genuine warmth of Ryan's childish affection.

She had to turn away so her heart wouldn't break. Closing the door behind Ryan and his foster mother, she reached into the closet for Blake's coat, fighting to hold on to her tears. Why couldn't Blake hear the truth in a child's words?

"I think Ryan knows daddy material when he sees it."

Silence was Blake's answer, his meaning all too clear.

Without looking up, she handed him his coat. "Thanks for your help with the kids. I'll bring you the final Nestlings report tomorrow morning. You can let yourself out."

Blake found her in the kitchen, standing outside the cocoon of light emanating from the black enamel hood over the cooking island. It wasn't like her to seek the comfort of enveloping darkness.

"Wren?"

At the sound of his voice, she whirled around. "Blake! What are you—?"

"I thought maybe a cup of coffee before I..." He took several steps across the black-and-white tiled floor, then stopped.

He'd tried to leave, he really had. He'd gone halfway down the front walk. But Ryan had called him Daddy and Wren had looked so sad, and he had to make it right with her, had to make her understand it was all an illusion.

"Of course. I'll just—"

"Let me. I know where everything is." He crossed to the coffeemaker beside her on the shiny white counter, but she sidestepped to the sink to fill the glass pot. He captured the black canister and spooned aromatic dark grounds into the filter, timing his moves so he'd meet her back at the appliance. But she refused to look at him, busied herself pouring water into the top while he slid the filter in and flipped the switch.

He stepped in front of her. "Wren, I... wanted to tell you what a great job you did on the Nestlings account. What a great job *we* did. We made a pretty good team."

Damn. It wasn't what he'd intended. He'd meant to praise her, but not to give her false hopes. He'd never worked closely with anyone. He was too consumed by the work itself, too intense... like the Colonel. Those were the very reasons people kept their distance.

Everyone except Wren.

"I thought so, too," she ventured, lifting her face with the familiar tilt of pride that boosted his spirits, until he saw light reflect from moisture on her cheeks.

Surely she hadn't been crying. In all her growing years, he'd never seen her cry. The prospect filled him with a sense of urgency.

"This afternoon added to the evidence."

"Evidence?" She looked perplexed, but her sadness didn't diminish.

Nor did his growing need to drive it away, no matter how foolhardy his words. "That we can work together well. Give and take. Help each other out. I thought we handled the kids like . . . partners."

The word didn't strike lightning, didn't cause the floor to quake. Out in the open, it was just another word that seemed to have lost all its threat.

He could still see caution in her, but she chanced a measuring look.

"Working partners," he coaxed.

That's what they'd been. That was all he could offer, what he *had* to offer if it would bring back the teasing to her eyes, if it would make her laugh. Suddenly he wanted very much to hear her laugh again.

"How many men and women do you know who can do all that together and produce a successful pot of coffee, too?"

A painful little smile was all she rallied before her head dipped.

"Not funny, huh?"

Her head nodded slowly from side to side, her mass of dark hair glowing with streaks of auburn and chestnut in the halo of light that encircled them.

What more could he say? They could work on coffee and clients together, but he cared too much about her to let her expect more. She deserved a home and family. No matter how much he wanted to make her happy, he wasn't the man to give those to her. What they'd shared this afternoon was an illusion. Wren couldn't know how much he wasn't daddy material.

But he remembered something from a man who had been.

"Bet you can't get to three without smiling." He said the words quietly, scavenging his memory to recall if they were right. If he didn't reach her now, he was afraid he might lose her. He didn't want to lose her.

Her head came up with a jerk. "What?"

"I said . . . I bet you can't go all the way to a count of three without—"

"Blake, I don't think—"

He raised a warning finger to quiet her, then touched it to her lips. "Ooonnneee . . ." He drew the word out solemnly, the only change in his face the exaggerated deepening of his frown.

"Twoooo . . ." He let devilment creep into his eyes then, challenging her, daring her to try to hold out against him. The palms of his hands grew damp as he watched her struggle between this rare downheartedness and the merriment that was never far from her lips. He knew then that if he had to resort to burlesque, he would.

Clasping her shoulders, he tilted his head, waggled his brows, let his smile spread. She peered up at him, her eyes wide with disbelief.

"Two and a haaalllfff . . ." He saw her yield, more a tentative surrender than a real smile, but it buoyed him as if he'd just cast off in a balloon.

Drawing in a deep breath, he whispered, "Two and three-quaarrrterrrsss," and watched reluctant whimsy spread across her face. He could feel her laughter start, a soft cascade that drew him like a parched man is drawn to an oasis.

He dipped his head, and her rippling amusement slid into a kind of purr as she went soft and pliant in his grasp. The sweet warmth of her breath played along his cheek, the rumble of his own chuckle faded as his mouth brushed hers.

Then everything stilled. Hot and thirsty, he sought her lips, tasting and savoring as if he could never get enough of her. He'd been lost in a desert, and he couldn't stop himself, wouldn't stop himself from drinking in her life-giving freshness, her wellspring of light.

He refused to come to his senses, fought against that damnable control, until her lithe body molded to his and she slid her hands up to cling to his neck. He knew then that control was no longer in his hands. Circling his arms around her, he drew her tight against him, letting her know she mustn't let him go away.

Kissing a path to her ear, he whispered, "A gambler should always know the stakes." He heard her breath catch as he explored the shallows behind her earlobe. She tasted of sweet lemon.

"A kiss?" she asked before she tugged his mouth back to hers, answering his explorations with the tip of her tongue.

"More than one," he murmured, drawing her nearer, aware of the eager press of her breasts against him and his own need growing against her. His hands began a slow descent down her back.

"How...many?" she managed between kisses, her breathing coming harder.

His hands slipped under the edge of her sweater and found something smooth and silky and warm from her heat. Beneath it, he could feel the firmness of her body, the subtle ridges of her ribs.

"How many...what?" He moved his hands up her sides until he could cup the curves of her breasts, but the satiny fabric kept him from her sleek warm skin.

He brushed his thumbs across its slippery texture and found her nipples taut and hard, like small berries, miniature peaks thrusting against the soft material, against the burnishing of his thumbs, evoking breathless mewlings that mingled with his growls.

"Kisses," she breathed into his mouth, her own hands seeking the hem of his sweater, and slipping underneath to tug at his T-shirt.

"Negotiable."

Somewhere far away, the sound of an opening door slowed his journey down the side of her neck.

"Let's negotiate." She kissed his chin, his cheek, nipped his earlobe, then blew into his ear.

The front door closed with a firm click, staying his hands. "Ruby," he whispered.

Wren pulled back just enough to look at him, her eyes still dark with passion but edged with the uncertainty he thought he'd routed.

"Does that mean negotiations are over?" she asked.

In the distance he could hear feet being stamped and the click of the closet door.

"Wren, I'm home." Ruby's voice pushed into their intimacy.

Sliding his hands to Wren's waist, he nibbled at her ear. "Would you consider my place?"

Footsteps sounded along the hall, drawing nearer, sending fingers of reality creeping into this haven he'd let himself share with Wren. Leaning down, he kissed her again, trying to hold on to the enchantment.

"Your place," Wren murmured against his mouth, sending a new wave of heat licking toward his groin.

"Wren, dear," Ruby called, "I forgot to tell you this afternoon. I have some good news." The footsteps stopped. "I talked to Blake's other shareholder. He wants you to call him."

With a snap, the overhead lights blazed on. "*Here* you are! I thought I smelled coffee."

As if executing a dance, Blake stepped back at the same moment Wren did. He stared at his aunt, who was busy pouring coffee at the counter. Then he stared back at Wren. Her face was stricken.

In the harsh light of Ruby's words, he saw that what had seemed an oasis had been only a mirage.

Chapter Twelve

"Ruby, what have you done now?" Wren demanded the minute she heard the front door snap shut, proclaiming Blake's departure. She caught the corner of her swollen lip in her teeth at the sight of Ruby's wide-eyed innocence. She hadn't meant to sound so upset, but this time Ruby had gone too far.

"Wren, dear, whatever do you mean?" Ruby carried two bright red mugs to the glass-topped kitchen table and sat down. "Come have your coffee, and let's talk about why that nephew of mine bolted out of here like a wild stallion."

"You know perfectly well why." Wren slumped down onto the black-and-white striped chair. "Your well-timed announcement made him think I'm after more of his company's shares."

"It won't hurt him to think that for a while."

Wren recognized the stubborn set of Ruby's jaw, so much like Blake's when he was on a mission. Yet there was a decided sparkle in her light blue eyes, while what she'd seen in Blake's when he'd stalked out of the house had been more like sparks. His mute departure still made her shiver.

Ruby circled an arthritic finger around the rim of her mug. "The truth is, Kyle Kramer called *me,* just like he always does every month or two. Such a charmer, that man." She rolled her eyes toward the ceiling. "He wanted to know about *you,* dear…wants to meet you. I suspect he wants to ask you out. Because of all that *Blake* told him about you." She puckered the corners of her mouth as if to say, "What do you think of *that?*" Then she took a sip of her coffee and watched Wren over the rim. "I expect Blake will find out soon enough, and it won't hurt him to know, either. That man needs to get his priorities right."

"*Ru-by…*" Wren murmured in frustration. How could she love this woman and be so exasperated with her at the same time? She stared into the glistening liquid in her own mug and wondered what Blake could have told Kyle Kramer that would make him want to ask her out.

"I'm afraid all you've done was remind Blake of what his priorities really are. It's pretty apparent that Brockman Incorporated, will always be number one with him." She fought to keep from sighing.

"Blake is an intelligent man, Wren. Has to be if he's going to call himself my nephew. But when it comes to matters of the heart, I've never seen anyone so slow.

"When you told me you'd decided not to buy the Bransons' shares, *I* decided I'd have to do something to get him moving."

"I can't buy Blake's approval, Ruby. He has to want me as a partner." Wren stopped fighting the sigh, her frustration giving way to wistfulness. She tried not to remember Blake's hungry kisses, his gentle hands tracing the curves of her body, moves he'd managed pretty well by himself until Ruby had interrupted. But that was all Blake's kisses had been—moves—not caresses born from matters of the heart. He wanted her, but he didn't love her.

"You got him moving all right... straight out the door." Her attempt at laughter came out as a catch in her throat.

"I'm sure you'll bring him to his senses, dear." Ruby reached across to pat her on the hand.

Could she? Even if she convinced Blake of Ruby's ploy, she knew things would never be the same between them. She thought they'd been sharing, building trust, but that had toppled like a tower of blocks with Ruby's intervention.

"Someday you'll thank me for doing you a favor."

Fairy godmothers granted wishes, Wren thought with a sinking heart, so how come she got a good-hearted gremlin for a matchmaker?

Much as she hated to admit it, Ruby probably had done her a favor. Blake might want her as a partner in bed, but she wanted him as a partner for life.

In spite of all they'd shared on the Nestlings account—all their funny experiences with the expectant parents, the wonderful play with the children—Ruby's manipulations had made one thing clear: the fortress Blake had built of Brockman Incorporated, still stood between them like the Great Wall of China.

* * *

Kyle Kramer. Wren was talking to Kyle Kramer! Blake whipped his four-by-four into the passing lane and raced through a yellow light. Kyle who owned the last twenty percent of his company.

"Damn!" Blake slammed his fist against the steering wheel, then swore again at the unintended beep of his horn.

He should have had such a blaring jolt earlier this afternoon—to alert him to dangerous conditions. Because that's what they'd been, from the minute he'd walked into Ruby's and found Wren there with Jaime and those children looking like a young family. There'd been dangerous conditions that had hooked into feelings he thought he'd managed to keep buried. At least he had, until Wren had grown up. Until, overnight, she'd become a woman, full of warmth and laughter and kisses sweeter than—

No. Until she'd become the owner of forty percent of his company... and out for another twenty percent.

His growl reverberated in his ears as he fishtailed into his drive. He stomped the brake and slithered to an angled stop not two inches from the garage.

Slamming the car door, he stormed up the walk, charging the steps two at a time. At the familiar second-floor condo, he yanked off his glove and dug into his pocket. The keys clinked in the muted quiet of the hall, a small sound that shook him like the tolling of a knell. The large silver key caught the hall light, gleaming as it swayed.

His reminder, his talisman to ward off illusions. But it wasn't working. Little Maddie had been charmed by the key's jingle, just as he'd been charmed by her kittenish smile. Just as he'd been captivated by Wren's throaty laughter.

Wren had called it a magic key. Today, for a brief enchanted hour or two, he'd let himself believe in magic.

Jamming the condo key into the lock, he flung the door open and strode across the darkened living room. He snatched up the portable phone from the coffee table and stood punching in the numbers, juggling the instrument between hands while he jerked his arms out of his jacket and flung it to a nearby chair.

"Kyle, if you're there, pick up. Don't avoid me. I know what's going—"

"Blake, what's up, buddy? You sound kinda ticked off."

"I'm more than kinda ticked off. What's the idea of talking to Wren about my shares without letting me know?"

"Whoa, hold on. First of all, if I'm not mistaken, I paid you genuine American greenbacks for those shares, old buddy, which I believe, under most circumstances, would make them *mine*. Am I right?"

"All right, all right, you know what I mean. The point is, you should have let me know she'd contacted you, that she was interested in buying. I want to make a counter—"

"She didn't, and as far as I know, she isn't."

"*What?*"

"Wren didn't contact me, Blake. I called her... to ask her out."

"You didn't talk about my shares?"

"*My* shares. As a matter of fact, I haven't talked to Wren. Yet. I got your aunt Ruby, and she said she'd have Wren call me."

Wren wasn't after his shares—*Kyle's* shares—Blake corrected impatiently. He paced around the coffee table trying to absorb the relief, at the same time a new surge of anger swept through him.

"You're going to ask her for a *date?*" Blake struggled to maintain control.

"Hey, bud, I figure any woman who has you as befuddled as you were when you were up here is worth checking out."

"You can't."

"I *can't?* What makes you think that, old buddy?"

Blake could hear Kyle's chortle, and he knew he should end the conversation right then. Instead, he plunged in headlong. "She's too young. Hardly more than a kid, I told you that. Not someone a thirty-year-old ski instructor should be asking out."

"If you'd said ski bum, I'd be right down there to punch you in that much-too-classic schnoz of yours. But I'm gonna overlook the implication, *plus* the fact that you're a good year older than me, *old* buddy. I realize you're fighting the green-eyed monster."

"What are you talking about?"

"You're jealous. You don't want me to ask her out. I think you're in love with the little gal!"

This time Kyle's chuckle held a clear edge of warmth, which was the one thing that kept Blake from sputtering. Kyle was serious. He was also crazy.

"I'm not—"

"And I suspect that whatever brought on this call means you owe her an apology."

Blake stood in stunned silence.

"Give it some thought, old buddy."

"Kyle, you should mind your own—"

Blake could still hear Kyle's laughter when the phone clicked in his ear.

"Damn!" He slammed the instrument down on the table. Some buddy. Kyle had no business asking Wren out. Accusing him of being jealous when all he was was...

Blake paced to the small efficiency kitchen and stood staring into space. He needed coffee. The sudden craving reminded him that he and Wren had never gotten to it at Ruby's. They'd been too engrossed in...other things. The memory of her eager kisses, of her body pressed against his, of the full tight peaks of her breasts beneath satiny fabric sent heat knifing through him. He felt himself respond just as he had with her in his arms, a compelling ache that he had no business feeling for her.

Willing himself into action, he crossed to the counter, where he measured out coffee and poured in water, but the gurgling brew and rising scent of hazelnut did little to waylay the direction of his thoughts.

He wanted her—it was that simple. But Kyle was crazy to accuse him of being in love. She was too young. She was his charge. She wanted little Maddies and Ryans running all over her life.

Pouring coffee into a large brown mug, he paced to the living room and sprawled into the puffy leather chair, gulping down swallows of the steamy liquid.

What Wren needed was to get on with her relationship with Jaime Sandoval. What *he* needed was to get back to Brockman Incorporated.

The thought stopped the mug in midair. This wasn't the first time in the past few weeks that the prospect of going back to the office felt empty. He sat forward, clasping the mug between his hands.

He'd focused all his drive on business, let his work override everything, just as he'd done in St. Louis. Just like the Colonel. And now it was coming up empty?

Suddenly he knew he didn't want to go back to the office and not hear Wren's bright laughter. He didn't want to spend hours crunching data and never see the teasing in her sweet cocoa eyes.

He didn't want her to leave Brockman Incorporated. But she would after his reaction tonight. Just as Cathleen Kohlmann had left.

He couldn't let that happen, not with Wren. Things with Wren were different. He clapped the coffee mug onto the table.

First thing tomorrow morning, he'd call her into his office and apologize.

Better yet, he'd call her tonight at Ruby's and offer her a full partnership.

He was on his feet now, searching the room for the discarded jacket. Snatching it from the floor, he shoved into the sleeves, patting the pockets. Where the hell had he put those keys? He couldn't see Wren without his magic key. And he couldn't wait until tomorrow.

All the windows in Ruby's house were dark. Sitting in his four-by-four in her drive, Blake peered at his watch by the dashboard lights. Ten-thirty, and they were already in bed?

For a moment he considered simply unlocking the front door and letting himself in. But Ruby had ears like a hawk, and he didn't want to try to answer all the questions he knew she'd bombard him with. Hell, he couldn't even answer them for himself.

Stepping out of the Rover, he closed the door quietly and crunched through the packed snow on the drive, all the while studying the apple tree that grew at the side of the wide front porch. It didn't look much different, maybe a little smaller than it had when he was a kid, but childhood memories always tended to be oversized and exaggerated.

Except for his recollections of Ruby's scoldings. Those he was sure weren't exaggerated. He grinned, imagining the elfin woman lecturing all six feet of him if she caught him climbing again.

Cutting across the front lawn, he high-stepped through the snow until he faced the exact center of the house. His room had been the first on the left, his window just a few feet away from the tree branches, but he was pretty sure Wren's was the one in the middle. If he could get up the slope of the porch roof, he could tap on her window....

That was as far as he let his thoughts project.

Tramping to the base of the tree, he looked up, measuring the likelihood of success. The divided trunk and familiar stair-step branches hadn't changed much except to grow thicker and more sturdy with the years.

Piece of cake. He would have to be a little more careful than he'd been on early summer evenings at thirteen. Climbing in snow-crusted loafers at thirty-one would be somewhat more of a challenge. In those days he'd been after a little excitement and the admiration of his friends. Tonight he sought a fair damsel. The thought made him smile.

Grabbing a branch above his head, he kicked the snow from his shoes and planted his feet in the juncture of the divided trunk, then hoisted himself up. Icy branches crackled with his weight, the pops rending the silence like gunshots. He winced, squatting very still as snow cascaded down the neck of his jacket.

Ice-cream cake, he thought wryly and shivered. He was going to have to get a move on or he'd freeze to death . . . or get arrested for failing to break-and-enter fast enough.

Grabbing a higher branch, he pulled, ignoring the icy snaps and a new onslaught of snow. He could see over the edge of the porch roof now, could measure the six-inch-deep slope of snow he'd have to traverse to get to the middle window. If he had his skis, he could sidestep right up.

The image deepened his smile. Reaching higher, he hauled himself level with the edge of the porch. Easy does it, now. Swipe a path clear of snow, brace a knee on the shingles, grab the frame of the storm window . . .

He reached out until his fingers gained purchase around the edge of the old wooden window frame. Good. Now to claim the summit.

Everything would have been fine if there hadn't been ice. The minute he felt his knee slip, he threw himself forward, lunging for the peak of the roof. With a muffled thump, he landed flat out, his fingers locked on to the ridge of shingles under the snow, keeping him from sliding icily—and unceremoniously—to the ground.

The sound of an opening window brought his face out of the snow that had muffled his groan. "Wren?" He prayed it was her at the same time he almost hoped it wasn't.

"Blake?" Her shocked voice echoed in the snowy quiet.

Thank God. "Shhh, you'll wake Aunt Ruby. Listen, could you just sort of reach out and give me a hand?"

"Blake, what are you *doing?*" Her voice was whispery with restraint, unintentionally seductive.

"I'm visiting you. But somebody forgot to clean off the damn roof." Also, it wasn't Kyle who was crazy. It was him. He was out of control.

He thought he heard a giggle, but he couldn't raise his head high enough to glare at her. Strangely, he didn't want to glare. He was having trouble keeping from grinning himself.

"There's a foothold over near the wall."

"Wren, there are no footholds on a shingled roof."

"Maybe not when you lived here, but there've been a few . . . structural improvements since then."

It irked him that he couldn't see the laughter in her eyes. He stuck out his leg, groping in the snow until his foot hit something solid. "You mean you—?"

"Boys aren't the only ones who climb trees. But I'll have to concede, I never made a snow angel up here. Wish I'd thought of it."

He could hear her laughing now, and it made him forget the cold wetness seeping through his clothes. Sliding toward the house, he braced his foot against whatever she'd anchored and relaxed his grip on the peak.

"Whenever your snow angel's done, you can climb up. There are slats like a ladder."

Puffing snow from his face, he found more footholds and, in seconds, scrambled to the peak. He perched there, full of exhilaration at the sight of Wren standing at the open window, her eyes wavering between delight and not-too-successful primness. A snow angel in a white flannel nightgown, except that its softness didn't hide her grown-up curves, and her wide moca eyes shone with feelings that were very much a woman's.

"Now that you're here, are you going to play the fiddle?"

She cocked her head quizzically, her rippling hair falling forward on her shoulder, stunning him again with the awareness that she was no longer a girl.

She wasn't in any hurry to offer him further assistance, either.

"Is that what I have to do to get you to let me in?" Because if it was, he knew, as surely as he knew winter melts into spring, that he would play until daffodils pushed up in the yard below if she asked him. He would make a song for this woman who brought him laughter and light. Who was bringing him back to life.

How else could he explain almost breaking his neck on a porch roof, in the snow, in the middle of the night?

One more word came to him then. Love. Love would do this to a man. Love would make a man crazy.

He was in love.

At sight of the silly grin spreading across Blake's face, Wren stepped back from the window. "I'm tempted to make you *sing* me a song, but I think the cold is freezing your brain. Maybe you'd better come in."

She knew she was making a mistake. She should point him back down the apple tree, back to earth and the solid ground of Brockman Incorporated, but she knew she couldn't send him away.

She watched him ease into her room and gain his footing before he brushed snow from the sill and closed the window. The sight of him caked with white from head to foot, his hair glistening dark gold with moisture, was more than she could bear.

"Don't move. I'll get some towels."

She'd only half turned before he grasped her waist with insistent hands and spun her back into his arms. She felt the cold nip of snow through her gown, the fierce heat of his mouth on hers, like fire and ice flashing through her, coming together somewhere deep inside to melt into wanting that was moist and warm.

For an instant her mind protested. There was no logic here, no caution, no defenses. She'd never seen him like this. But she'd seen it in him, the intensity, the passion she'd dreamed he'd share someday with her. Could she bear to know his passion without his love?

A knock sounded at the door, and Blake's mouth stilled, though his arms held her close against him.

"Wren, I heard noises." Ruby's words from the other side of the door were more curious than worried.

She peeked up at him, almost unable to contain her laughter at the alarm on his face, at his emphatic gesturing.

"It's just Blake." She almost chortled, watching his eyes widen, feeling him loosen his hold as if readying to head for the apple tree. Grabbing his belt loops, she relished his sharp intake of breath. Silence followed.

"Oh. Well, good night then."

Wren couldn't help a tiny snort as she muffled her laughter against his chest.

"I don't believe it!" he whispered into her hair.

The scent of damp wool and warm masculinity filled her nostrils, making her want to tug his mouth back to hers, to tug him to her bed and make wild outrageous love with him before the sun came up and he came to his senses and flew back to the safety of his fortress.

Instead, she stepped out of his embrace, into a sudden lonely chill. "At the risk of asking the obvious, what are you doing here?"

"I came to offer you a job."

She took another step back, her heart tumbling. "I thought I already had a job."

"After the way I acted this evening, I thought you might resign."

She let the silence lengthen. "I've been considering it."

"Wren, you can't. I won't accept your resignation. With Roberta and Ernie's shares, you own as much of Brockman Incorporated, as I do."

"I decided not to buy their shares."

"But why? You beat me. Damned good job, too."

Even in the shadows of the room, she saw ironic pleasure deepen his smile. He moved closer.

"You have to buy the shares."

Her feet seemed to have fused to the floor because she couldn't move when he closed the gap between them.

"I want you as a full partner."

"A full—?"

His mouth settled onto hers, wiping away her astonishment. His hands found her waist and tugged her against the hardness of his body, waking memories of dreams that had shimmered through her for so long. Cold moisture thrilled her fingers where she touched the heat of his neck.

"You make work fun," he breathed into her ear. "You make everything fun. Especially this."

She couldn't find breath to argue, wouldn't have if she could. She kissed him back, savoring the dusky flavor of coffee and hazelnuts, stilling the questions that prodded her heart.

"Besides—" he kissed her nose "—with you as my partner, I'll have more time." A trail of delicious tingling followed the kisses he traced to her ear. "I've been thinking of some other activities I'd like to engage in."

"Oh." She dipped her head. He was still talking business. Then the possibilities behind his words sank in, and her head shot up.

"Now hold on. Don't get your feathers up. I have something for you." He bent to kiss her again, a soft lingering kiss that she couldn't refuse because she'd dreamed of this too long.

Taking her hand in his, he opened her fingers one by one and laid his shiny silver key in her palm. "This is for you."

She stared down at the token, unexpectedly warm against her skin. What did it mean? A part of his business and all the worries that went with it?

She'd always thought of it as the key to his heart. Was that what he was offering her now?

She searched his face and found that rare smile that dented the corners of his mouth, the evanescent whimsy that turned her resistance, if she had any at all, to stardust.

That was when she knew what to ask. "Does it still have magic in it?" His face went serious, and for the first time, she saw uncertainty in his eyes.

"I don't know." His hand came to her cheek, touching her gently as if to keep her there. "A lot of it got used this afternoon. On a little bit of a thing called Maddie and a scalawag named Ryan." He drew in a long breath. "And on a hardheaded guy who finally understood just how much love he learned in this house." He paused again, as if trying to give words to something he understood best in his heart.

"I know you kind of lost out on a mother, Wren. And the Colonel was too busy to be my father. But we both had Ruby."

The words were a plea. He was asking her to understand his fortresses. He was telling her he was willing to give them up, to take a chance.

But she was afraid to trust the thunder she heard. Was it truly his crumbling defenses and not just her racing heart?

"What if the magic's all used up?" she whispered.

"I think magic is like love...you can't use it up. You just have to say the right words."

"Words like *abracadabra?*" Blake would need that kind of magic.

"Words like, *I love you, Wren. I want you to be my wife.*"

This was a dream. "Those are powerful words." She stalled, waiting to feel his hand slip away and see him break and run as he had before.

Instead, he curled a knuckle under her chin, tilting her head to look into his deep blue eyes. His smile was back in place, unguarded.

"Powerful magic." He bent to steal a kiss from her half-open lips. "This key will fit the door of a wonderful house, a house full of love. And a nursery full of babies," he added, grinning. "All you have to do is say the word."

"Babies?" Now she knew she was dreaming. Except that the length of his body against hers felt very real, and the beating of his heart matched hers. "You want me to say words that will make a nursery full of *babies?"*

"You don't *like* babies?" He looked shocked.

The question echoed in her memory, producing a smile that she tried to cover with a scowl. The attempt wasn't very successful. Tucking in her chin, she squinted up at him.

"What I think about babies in irrelevant, Mr. Brockman. We have a business to run, and if I'm going to be a full partner, I want everybody working on the airport account so we can build Brockman Incorporated, into a—"

"Wr-en."

He cut her off with a kiss, but she heard the familiar downswing of warning in his voice. Yet his time he didn't sound like an impatient big brother, didn't look like a grumpy old guardian. What he looked like was just plain sexy.

"Love me, Wren," he said between kisses.

"I always have."

"Marry me." He kissed her again.

She would do that, too, because it would take a lifetime to share all the love Aunt Ruby had taught them both. Which reminded her...

"I think we should elope down Ruby's apple tree."

"Mmm." His lips tickled hers with an answer that was as much kisses as words. "Good idea. Then we can start working on Babies Incorporated."

She pulled back just enough to gaze into his laughing eyes. "*Babies* Incorporated?" Dreams did come true. "I like it. I think we have real partnership potential here."

Magic words, said with love-filled laughter. After that they were too busy sealing the partnership to say more.

* * * * *

Silhouette celebrates motherhood in May with...

Debbie Macomber
Jill Marie Landis
Gina Ferris Wilkins

in

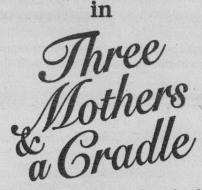

*Three
Mothers
& a Cradle*

Join three award-winning authors in this
beautiful collection you'll treasure forever.
The same antique, hand-crafted cradle
connects these three heartwarming romances,
which celebrate the joys and excitement of
motherhood. Makes the perfect gift for yourself
or a loved one!

A special celebration of love,

Only from 🔺 *Silhouette*®

—where passion lives.

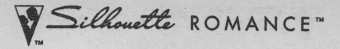

Silhouette ROMANCE™

Arriving in April from Silhouette Romance...

Bundles of JOY

Six bouncing babies. Six unforgettable love stories.

Join Silhouette Romance as we present these heartwarming tales
featuring the joy that only a baby can bring!

THE DADDY PROJECT by Suzanne Carey
THE COWBOY, THE BABY AND THE RUNAWAY BRIDE
by Lindsay Longford
LULLABY AND GOODNIGHT by Sandra Steffen
ADAM'S VOW by Karen Rose Smith
BABIES INC. by Pat Montana
HAZARDOUS HUSBAND by Christine Scott

Don't miss out on these BUNDLES OF JOY—only from Silhouette Romance.
Because sometimes, the smallest packages can lead to the biggest surprises!

And be sure to look for additional BUNDLES OF JOY
titles in the months to come.

BOJ1

Silhouette ROMANCE™

is proud to present

WRANGLERS & Lace

The spirit of the West—and the magic of romance…Saddle up and get ready to fall in love Western-style with WRANGLERS AND LACE. Starting in May with:

Daddy Was a Cowboy
by Jodi O'Donnell

Jamie Dunn was determined to show Kell Hamilton she was the best ranch hand he'd ever hired. But what would her handsome boss do when he learned she had another full-time career—as a mother?

Wranglers and Lace: Hard to tame—impossible to resist—these cowboys meet their match.

SL-1

Five unforgettable couples say "I Do"... with a little help from their friends

Always a Bridesmaid!

Always a bridesmaid, never a bride...that's me, Katie Jones—a woman with more taffeta bridesmaid dresses than dates! I'm just one of the continuing characters you'll get to know in ALWAYS A BRIDESMAID!—Silhouette's new across-the-lines series about the lives, loves...and weddings—of five couples here in Clover, South Carolina. Share in all our celebrations! (With so many events to attend, I'm sure to get my own groom!)

In June, **Desire** hosts
THE ENGAGEMENT PARTY by Barbara Boswell

In July, **Romance** holds
THE BRIDAL SHOWER by Elizabeth August

In August, **Intimate Moments** gives
THE BACHELOR PARTY by Paula Detmer Riggs

In September, **Shadows** showcases
THE ABANDONED BRIDE by Jane Toombs

In October, **Special Edition** introduces
FINALLY A BRIDE by Sherryl Woods

Don't miss a single one—wherever
Silhouette books are sold.

▼ *Silhouette®*
TM

AAB-G

SILHOUETTE... Where Passion Lives

Don't miss these Silhouette favorites by some of our most distinguished authors! And now, you can receive a discount by ordering two or more titles!

SD#05844	THE HAND OF AN ANGEL by BJ James	$2.99	☐
SD#05873	WHAT ARE FRIENDS FOR?	$2.99 U.S.	☐
	by Naomi Horton	$3.50 CAN.	☐
SD#05880	MEGAN'S MIRACLE	$2.99 U.S.	☐
	by Karen Leabo	$3.50 CAN.	☐
IM#07524	ONCE UPON A WEDDING		
	by Paula Detmer Riggs	$3.50	☐
IM#07542	FINALLY A FATHER by Marilyn Pappano	$3.50	☐
IM#07556	BANISHED by Lee Magner	$3.50	☐
SSE#09805	TRUE BLUE HEARTS		
	by Curtiss Ann Matlock	$3.39	☐
SSE#09825	WORTH WAITING FOR by Bay Matthews	$3.50	☐
SSE#09866	HE'S MY SOLDIER BOY by Lisa Jackson	$3.50	☐
SR#08948	MORE THAN YOU KNOW		
	by Phyllis Halldorson	$2.75	☐
SR#08949	MARRIAGE IN A SUITCASE		
	by Kasey Michaels	$2.75	☐
SR#19003	THE BACHELOR CURE by Pepper Adams	$2.75	☐

(limited quantities available on certain titles)

AMOUNT	$_____
DEDUCT: 10% DISCOUNT FOR 2+ BOOKS	$_____
POSTAGE & HANDLING	$_____
($1.00 for one book, 50¢ for each additional)	
APPLICABLE TAXES*	$_____
TOTAL PAYABLE	$_____
(check or money order—please do not send cash)	

To order, complete this form and send it, along with a check or money order for the total above, payable to Silhouette Books, to: **In the U.S.:** 3010 Walden Avenue, P.O. Box 9077, Buffalo, NY 14269-9077; **In Canada:** P.O. Box 636, Fort Erie, Ontario, L2A 5X3.

Name:_____

Address:_____ City:_____

State/Prov.:_____ Zip/Postal Code:_____

*New York residents remit applicable sales taxes.
Canadian residents remit applicable GST and provincial taxes.　　SBACK-MM

Silhouette®